When Souls Make Love

Maverick Prem

Leadstart
INKSTATE

ISBN 978-93-89759-82-2
Copyright © Maverick Prem, 2020

First published in India 2020 by Inkstate Books
An imprint of Leadstart Publishing Pvt Ltd

Sales Office:
Unit No.25/26, Building No.A/1,
Near Wadala RTO,
Wadala (East), Mumbai – 400037 India
Phone: +91 969933000
Email: info@leadstartcorp.com
www.leadstartcorp.com

Disclaimer: The views expressed in this book are those of the Author and do not pertain to be held by the Publisher.

Editor: Shayoni Mitra
Cover: Ami Parekh
Layouts: Kshitij Dhawale

ALetterofGratitude

'Acknowledgement section' they said, and I chose to call it 'A letter of gratitude'. I feel that sounds more apt, for it is not just about acknowledging, but truly celebrating this moment. Of everything, I feel grateful to this space you and me are in. Amidst all the societal expectations, work pressure, mortgage loans, television ads, Netflix series, seasonal sales, Instagram notifications, and more that fills your day with, you are present here for the love of reading, holding this book in hand. This to me is more important than anything. The space we share here is important. Talking about space, I am not talking about how close we are but how far we are. Proximity spoils the bigger picture, whereas distance defines the view. From here, however far or close you are, I take the pleasure to look at the way you are holding this book. There is music in the way your fingers touch this book, and I can hear it in the way your eyes move through every word. Thank you for being in this moment, and realizing the preciousness of the now. It means a lot to me, and to you too. Can we call this mutual?

Ok, now coming to the long list of happy souls that I want to thank over. Go forward only if you have the time to spend and buy my gratitude. The list looks like this:

My Mom and Dad – for letting me be

1st standard Tamil Miss - Latha - my first crush

2nd standard student - Priya – my second crush

Tamilselvan Periappa, Konangi Periyappa, Boopathy Sithappa, Madhi Athai, Pandian Sithappa, Baskar Mama, Senthil Mama, Sethu Mama, Velusamy Thatha, Padmavathi Aachi, Saraswathi Aachi, Sanmugam Thatha who carried me on their shoulders.

Madhurakavi Bhaskara Das - My soul's father and angel

Lillian and Roselyn – my best friends

Yuha – my talented sister who is just my opposite yet resonates when it matters

Karthi, Siddhu, Deepa, Kumar, Muthu – my roots

10th standard English Mam - Shobhana Selvam – who made me believe in my originality when it comes to writing in English

Maths teacher - Rathinaraj – for making me believe in the beauty of numbers

Physics Tuition teacher - Elango – who made me love the science of life

The soul I fell in love with at College – who remains what she is to me

Mythili – the sister from another womb, but connected deeper than it looked

MBA teacher - Ashwin Bhatia – who made me realize the free spirit in me

Caldwell Velnambi – my mentor, who saw the creator in me

Shyam – my partner with whom I evolved with, watching 'Fight Club' and 'Revolver'

The soul I rose in love with, Shindhu – my wife they say, but the friend I live with I'd say. My source, support, and serendipity

Thiagarajan – 'My father in love' I say, 'father in law' they say; who breathes books

Vani – 'my mother in love' I say, 'mother in law' they say; who gave me that first push to quit everything and start writing

Arjun, Pattu – My partners in crime with whom I share a very warm vibe with

Shankar Vanavarayar – my understanding without an explanation and connection beyond words

Vishwanath – my captain who taught me the onus of discipline and outcomes

Amar Ramesh & Nethra – the inspiring unicorns of purpose and dedication

Team Studio A - The friends at work who mean a family to me

Kuppu – one who taught me the power of pain, time, and priorities

My three-year-old son Theo Sakya – who questions and redefines everything

Tamizhachi – a magical soul who continues to bless me unconditionally

Suchi – the youngest soul who teaches me resilience and character, and the two leaves dancing in the breeze – denoting everything that there is to life

Each and everyone here have an impact in my life in their own way. It is one love and one life that we share together. There are endless souls I'd have forgotten to mention here. We can fight about that in person. For now, let us love this moment of gratitude. Thank you!

AboutTheAuthor

He dreamt to become a doctor, studied to become an engineer, aspired to become an Entrepreneur and ended up as a creative writer. Maverick Prem is an avid reader of people and nature, and draws inspiration from the simple everyday things he finds around. A firm believer in the magic of the universe, he has always taken life on the go and relishes the flow of instincts. He is currently working with Studio A, and is into creative writing, brand management, and documentary filmmaking. "When Souls Make Love" is his first book that revolves around the love that exists in the generation today.

Contents

1.   The End   08

1.5. When Stars Talk   15

2.   Souls Inked   18

3.   The Train of Memories   37

3.5. Stars being human   62

4.   Can Love Happen twice?   64

5.   Love in (and) Lust   77

5.5. The Flow in our Stars   92

6.   Intensity of Innocence   94

6.5. The Bigger Picture   136

7.   The Turning Point   139

8.   Into the Woods   146

8.5. Almost there   167

9.   Wild Love   168

9.5. When Souls Make Love   189

10.   The Beginning   199

Chapter 1

The End

"One moment I feel like we just got married. And the next moment I feel like we have been married forever," he said, stirring his drink. He was okay with any drink, but was very particular about the glass he held. It had to merge with his mood, or he simply wouldn't raise a toast or hold the glass in the first place.

The one that he was holding then was a retro whiskey glass. It had a fine texture of leaf patterns engraved at its base that reflected the colour of the drink inside. To him, it was always about celebrating the subtle things, and the finesse that comes with them. Saturday nights were usually lit with spirits, but that night went sober. He had poured hot water into his glass, for the love of its warmth. He enjoyed the surprise that the sip of hot water gave to his lips.

Sitting by the side of the new coffee table set they had just bought, he took a sip, looking at her like he had when they started loving each other. That was 7 years ago. And they had been married for 4 years. They'd had everything between them. They travelled a lot, watched great movies, talked about powerful books, enjoyed fixing each other's drinks, renewed their wilderness through fights, relived the songs of the 80s and 90s, and the list goes on.

They were the kind of couple that people termed 'ideal' and 'made-for-each other' and with all the other fancy words. Yup, they were that, at least to the world. As two individuals who were crazy about each other, they had more memories than dreams to share with each other.

She was walking into the living room after folding and arranging the washed clothes in the respective cupboards in the bedroom. "So tell me, what do you think about this coffee table?" She asked, as she sat down with a sigh. It had been a long day that just didn't seem to stand still, for both of them, at work and at home, too. Life gets surprisingly busy when two people live together.

"I think you heard me. What do you think about the coffee table?" she asked again, this time slower and louder to get his attention. He seemed lost in thoughts.

It was a dark teakwood table, about 2 feet high. It came with 4 small wooden stools, but they bought just the table to cut down a little on the cost. Small or big, a saving is a saving – especially to the confused millennials who got to understand the importance of it lately. Also, both of them had been having a debate about buying that coffee table set ever since they spotted it at Home Centre.

To him, it simply seemed too expensive for being a coffee table that just wouldn't move anywhere. He loved to be on the move and feel the related experiences rather than spend on static materials. He was an ardent fan of movies like 'Fight Club', and 'Revolver'. That probably explained his reluctance and gave the context.

His attention to detail was in living every moment intensely and artistically. He wouldn't worry much even if he lost his wallet with his money and all his original identification cards. At the end of the day, he would call it an experience and vouch for its worth in the flow of life.

She was logical and different, though. She had a very astute taste for life. She loved experiences and products equally. Be it the dresses in the wardrobe or the desktop icons, she wished to keep things in order. She was bold and confident, yet vulnerable during sensitive situations. She was ready for adventure and excitement anytime, but was not a fan of the extremes.

She was well organized, and the better soul in the relationship that seemed real. Sophistication was her pursuit, and her belief was that life should progress with style and statement. He was the chaos and she was the order; he was rudderless and she was the compass... Both had their differences and that was precisely what kept them hooked.

"Well, it is not that I didn't hear you. It is just that I was expecting you to answer to my statement about marriage before that," he smirked and continued to stir his drink, taking the last sip of water that had lost its heat already.

"What marriage?"

"Our marriage..."

"Of course I know that. I mean, what about our marriage?"

"How can I make you understand?"

"By trying, maybe."

"I want you to interpret this feeling that I am having of late. One moment I feel like we just got married. And the next moment I feel like we have been married forever. It is like I can't get enough out of you, and I have had enough of you to last a lifetime. Light and shadow, smiles and tears, yes and no. Do you get me? What do you think of this?"

"You sound like you are drunk."

"Really?"

"You sound like it," she said, and stood up to stretch a little.

The time was 10 past 11 at night. It had been quite a while since they had sat together for a conversation. You can't blame them much, because their routines are wired to an insane cycle of duties, like most of our lives.

He was a creative writer in a top-notch firm. He took care of content and brand communication. His love for work only demanded more of him, and it got meaner when it came to the time he had for her. There was nothing to complain about work. But it required most of his concentration and mind space.

Naturally, coming home with a worked out mind, all he wanted to do, was love and be loved. Also, his dream was to become a writer and express his heart with words. It was very little time that he got for his wife or anyone else, much less himself.

She, on the other end, was fighting the most difficult battle on earth – being a working wife. She had to cook, make sure that the house chores were in order, the bills were paid, the clothes ironed, the floor clean, lights switched off when not in use, and... it never really ends, the list – doesn't it? On top of this, she was working in an IT firm that sucked her energy with long working shifts and longer commute times.

She had a round of thoughts running inside her head, given her fixed gaze on things in the room. She did that when she was deep in thoughts – look at things with fixated intervals. The room was filled with the grainy noise of absolute silence.

"Know what? This is more than just the coffee table. I think we need to talk," she said, and looked into his eyes.

It is always a tough task to confront the eyes of a woman who knows what she is talking about, and has thought over her words.

"Of course I think the same, too. This is about our marriage that I am talking about, and you are still stuck with this silly table that you fancied having in our living room," he said in a firm tone that sounded like he was registering a fact rather than replying.

"Oh, now you want to argue over something I so happily bought for both of us, is it?" She asked, her voice becoming louder.

"No, not at all. As I said, it is much more than that. I am talking about us, and you are still harping on about the table. What does that say, goddammit?" He shouted.

"Nothing. I don't want to say a thing more." She retreated and folded her hands.

Now that meant war. When a woman retreats, it only means there is more coming ahead rather than the momentary peace. Women just don't give up, unless it is in love or out of love. They are free spirits. He knew her better than anybody else.

Sticking to the basic instincts, he stated, "That's fine. You need not say anything. How often have you said the right thing when it mattered?"

He knew it was not exactly true. She was more sensible than him. But in the heat of the moment, it is always the ego that takes precedence.

"So you're saying that I don't matter?" She asked.

"No. I just said what you say doesn't sound right, at times," he replied instantly, without thinking.

"That's sad to hear."

"That didn't feel happy either, when I said it."

"What do you want?"

"What do you need?"

"I want respect."

"I need you to understand."

"I want you to understand, too... My feelings and my tears."

"Ah, the crying element! Can you please not start?"

"Will you just stop?"

That was it. They were both fuming at the moment. What started as a casual, laidback conversation was bringing out the ugly truth that lay inert in every relationship nowadays. Opposite poles do attract, but that doesn't take away the fact that they are different in their individual natures. Once in a while, the difference does raise its head, and the magnets fall apart. Fights happen, only to increase the attraction with all the friction that caused the fight.

But this time around, there was a new air of uncertainty that they both felt. Opposite poles were not attracting, but were staring at each other with folded arms.

"Ok, I am sorry," he said, but didn't mean it. "I know it is not the right thing to raise hell out of heaven. I don't know what we are fighting for, or what we are trying to prove to each other. What I do know is that love is all I have for you. And whatever it is that we started now, let us put it to an end."

Even before he could finish, she was already having words to spill. "I think that's the problem... the fact that we overlook a problem to make peace at that moment. We both know we've had bigger fights than this, but none of them last more than a night. We simply have not lived a day with grudges in our minds. I think *that's* the problem. Do you think we should have taken the time to fight properly to realize things from the heart, and know what the *other person wants*, rather than surpass the difficulty in it for the comfort of the moment?"

She had a point, and he was nodding in agreement. "What can I do?" He asked in a composed tone.

"The question should be, 'What should *we* do?'" She said, her forefinger tapping the coffee table. Before he could reply, she went to the kitchen, fetched herself a glass of water, and returned to the table. They both sat in silence.

But this wasn't the noisy grain of absolute silence. There was something else between the noise and the silence that they couldn't grasp. They let the moment prevail. The only sound in the room was of her gulping the water. She kept the glass on the coffee table with a thud that would have almost broken it.

He was looking into his glass morosely, and she was pressing her nails onto her palms. Lost in contemplation, they sat still and the few minutes that passed by, felt like an eternity.

Usually, he would have broken the silence and uttered a few words. But strangely, he kept quiet, not feeling the urge to talk. She came forward and just when she was about to say something, he stood up with a sigh and went into the bedroom.

It is funny how our egos play. He kept meddling with the pillow and bedsheet with his uncertain mood. In a while, she came to bed too, and carefully eased herself onto the other side. He kept looking at the wall on his side. The red and blue curtains were moving to the fan's whirls of air.

He couldn't sleep. Nor could she. It burnt them to digest the mood in the air and try to fall asleep when there was no sleep in the eyes. They were lying on the same bed, facing the opposite sides. It felt like the snow on one side and sunshine on the other, the way it happens in Iceland.

They had all the opportunities to talk to each other. It was just the two of them in the world that mattered then. All it took was a turn and a gaze to tune their worlds in. But they didn't. Two souls in love had just fought, and they needed salvation.

The universe was ready to embrace them and show them the light. But they took their time to go through the pain of this night. The way that ignorance is bliss and from the wisdom that the darkness yields, they were into it for the rest of the night, together, but alone.

And they did slip into sleep, after a long while, that only the stars can quantify. The universe took a step back slowly. The view from the top went far above, until the stars that watched these two souls resting, broken in pieces.

Chapter 1.5

When Stars Talk

"I told you that this was bound to happen. And it has, today," said the pink star with a smile that demanded acknowledgment.

"You did! But how I wished it hadn't happened at all," ranted the blue star. Both of them were watching the conversation in progress. If you are wondering what the stars are doing here, well, let us have the clouds clear. Each of us has a star that watches over us from the above. It makes sure we get what we need at the right time, and in the right place.

They are the adjustment bureaus of our destiny. They have a plan for each one of us. But the sweet spot is that, the only phase that they can't control is when we are in love. The stars just don't matter when two people are in love. All they could do is sit and watch. So the pink star was his confidant, and the blue star was her confidant. They were puzzled over what would happen after what had happened.

"Hey blue, so what do you think is going to happen now?" Pink asked.

"No idea, pink. We have to wait and watch. These humans have everything in place, but when it comes to love why do they lose control?" blue wondered.

"Isn't that what love is all about?"

"You mean to lose control?"

"No, I mean losing oneself. Only when you are lost can you find yourself. Often, there needs to be an empty space for the breeze to come in. So much clutter I say, there's so much clutter in human lives that there is no space for anything good to come into their lives. Let alone love!"

"Come on! Let us not speak in general. Let us talk about them in particular, these souls we look after."

"Of course, it applies to them too, very much… Take him, for instance. The fellow is good at heart. Agreed. But doesn't he have to be empathetic to her?"

"I thought he was… Or am I wrong?"

"You are neither right nor wrong. That's how these two have been. I mean, this guy is close to his own self, so close that he acts selfishly at times. That's one consequence of self-awareness. It becomes an obsession at times, and blocks your eyes from seeing beyond yourself. Self-awareness becomes self-centeredness pretty quickly."

"And her… I think she is one fine lady, but just that she swings her mood between logic and magic often. She loved him for the same things that she is now fighting against. Earlier, she loved this relentless romanticism and unpredictability in him, but now she asks for stability in the way he holds life. The way he holds her alone should matter. Everything else is a matter of gravity, right? Is she not supposed to love him with all the flaws that he has, just like how he loves her with all the scars that she has?"

"Flaws and scars are two different things."

"But the pain is the same, isn't it? At different points of time, the pain is there in both of them."

"Pain is inevitable, and has to be experienced rather than… wait, they are making a move. Let us watch what they are going to do."

"As their bodies rest their case, their souls are getting ready to play their roles now."

"Souls are always up, connected and characteristic."

"You know what the souls do when the mortal minds have a fight, right?"

"Yes!"

"They write letters…"

"To each other…"

"Until they come to an understanding…"

"That need not be an agreement..."

"But a clear understanding, nevertheless."

"That will cocoon them together."

"Oh yeah! We are in sync. Aren't we, blue?"

"Of course, pink!"

"Now let's raise a shine to it, and watch what happens!"

They twinkled together as the souls started contemplating.

Remember how, sometimes, you feel familiar with a person whom you had just met? Like you always feel close to a person however far you are, the way how the mere presence of someone makes you feel comfortable and reassured, you feel like you have had the most complete conversation with a person without having spoken a word, and silence brings an understanding between two souls after an argument...

These are instances beyond explanation, ones that make you feel magical. If you look closely, not many words are spoken at these instances but only silence thrives. You call it a vibe or frequency. Truth to be told, our souls are writing letters to each other all the time. That's why we feel familiar, positive, reassured, and real, even before we speak out to each other at times.

All those unspoken words, thoughts and feelings get translated into vibes, and are exchanged as letters. These letters are more powerful than spoken words. They come to the fore profoundly when earthly bodies can't come to terms with a situation. This was one such situation that was not just about the coffee table, but also more importantly, about two souls in love that had been hampered over time by modernization. They needed a conversation. They needed to write to each other, the troubled souls, and they did.

Chapter 2

Souls Inked

H E: (Getting drenched on the terrace with you)

I am sorry.

I am sorry that I made you go through this. Somehow, our last conversation had a profound impact on me. I wouldn't call it a scar, for it still hurts. I am not done with the pain yet. It hurts really bad, and makes me think. The words we spoke, and most importantly, those we didn't speak, they all account for the realizations we came to.

There is no doubting the love we have for each other. Our love is too precious. It has always been the bridge between us, ever since we knew each other. We never needed to live as one, but co-existed as two souls respecting each other's space, connected by a love to share this life together. Somehow, we had this notion that marriage was not essential and when two people loved each other, that was all it took to live together.

We consented to our parents' wish for getting us married. But I think we imbibed each other into our lives way before that. My history of understanding you rooted from the moment when we had not even met. I am talking about destiny.

There is this old Chinese proverb that says, 'An invisible red thread connects those who are destined to meet, regardless of time, place, or circumstance. The thread may stretch or tangle, but will never break.'

We are those entangled souls in love. We had and have so much love, but then, what possibly could create such a large crack between us that has extended up until now? No matter what, our problems were usually sorted out even without talking about them. And you know what? You were right about one thing. I think I had not handled our fights wisely.

Truth be told, I was always the one who apologized first when we fought, but had I ever realized my mistake to the fullest every time I apologised? That is a question to ponder. We love each other so much that we do not want to hurt each other in any way. We both had grown so close to each other that we were failing to see the individuals that we originally were.

'Two souls, one love' is amazing as a concept but are we losing our self-identity in the process of becoming a single unit? I don't know. What is love? Like a fish in the water, unaware of its surroundings, I truly do not know how to define the love that surrounds us. Figuratively speaking there are finite reasons of why we liked each other and what we didn't like in each other.

But there is something beyond these logical explanations that binds two (or more) souls together in the form of love. I felt that with you, hands down. We had left a lot behind us to live together. After all the years of love, passion, perseverance, sacrifice, memories, and dreams, how can the fire fade? We have heard people say this so often, that love fades after marriage gradually. Is it true? Are we responsible for that?

I mean, there is this way that you see me through your eyes. Wherever I am, whatever we are doing, even amidst a million people, that look from you uniquely pierces through me and makes me realize that magical, inexplicable feeling that I hold for you. Likewise, there is this way I kiss you unconditionally, somewhere from the bottom of my soul, touching not just your lips but your soul's layers effortlessly.

There is a way you let me be myself, even when it is not what you'd like. I can go on, and say so many little things that I now feel are fading slightly. Yes, life's buzz got the best of us. I agree with that. Is it because we are comfortable that we have each other always? Or the confidence that we are not going to drift apart anyway?

It feels we know what we are talking about, but there is more to it! How do I reckon it? How do I get even with that realization? How do I make sure I don't mess up with your heart again, luring you into this attractive chaos that riddles away your peace? How can I rewind? How can I unlearn? How can I be more? How can I get things back to the way they were? - Careless, loving, innocent and intense! I don't know. But what I do know is that I am a self-centred narcissist who thinks that he cares and knows about love, but is actually a bit too shallow to realize that he is not so. So many questions and too many confrontations...

"What should we do?"

You asked the right question. Somehow I am reminded of September 8, 2014, when we were watching the stars, lying on our terrace. Somehow I wish we could go back to that conversation and finish it up. Or rather, continue it endlessly.

"This is magical, the way we are lying next to each other and staring at the universe. The way our shoulders touch now seems far more mystical than those million constellations that keep expanding in front of us. What is this touch of yours that melts my existence into you and makes me feel crazy?" I asked, having lost my sense of time.

"I know you are smiling now. I can identify even when we are not looking at each other. I always know when you smile," you said with a smile that I could feel, too.

"I too felt the touch, of our toes brushing each other. There are the shoulders, yeah, but somehow all my attention has been focused on those tickling touches. Leave the stars. Let them be in peace. I am here with you. I am here for you!"

"This won't fade, will it?"

"Which one?"

"This one!"

"You mean this moment?"

"Yes, and the ones to come..."

"Of course, we will grow in love... We will grow young in love."

"What if it fades?"

"Come on, why would it?"

"What if this magic fades, like they say it does after marriage?"

"Well, I am sure it will never fade for us. But if it does, we can always light it up."

"With?"

"US!"

"Really?"

"Why would you doubt that?"

"Because I question it, doesn't mean I doubt that. It just means I'd love to listen to you talking to me."

"I love listening to you too. Listening is the best part of any conversation, especially in the ones where you don't have to convince the other person."

"And not to forget the lack of necessity to be ready with an impressive reply!"

"I like the way we sound when we talk about these little things that matter. The kind of effort that the heart takes to trickle these words to the brain, where they fail to accept any logic, and trickle down to the same place – the heart, and out into the wilderness of this friction that our breaths hold. I can feel it in our hands, yes, I can feel our breaths in our hands..."

"Gosh, conversations are something, aren't they?"

"Dope!"

"You are my drug."

"You are my headache."

"Intense."

"Really Intense, too."

"Do we complement each other?"

"Does it matter?"

You were all smiles, and I was about to reply with what I had in my mind, but suddenly, it rained. The first drop of the water from the faraway cloud touched us but we did not scramble upwards. Neither did we speak, nor did we care to continue the conversation that had been flowing seamlessly.

We got drenched.

In the sound of the rain, we kissed and basked in each other's warmth on the concrete floor that was kissing the falling rain. We didn't get up until one of us sneezed during the kiss. How is that even possible, I still wonder? Not the sneeze, but the kiss that feels wet on my lips even now.

Memories flash. That's their nature. All I can do is try to go back and complete the conversation that was left hanging in the air. I feel it would change things. Maybe everything else after that would add up to a different moment now. In fact, I am ready to do anything to change things between us. I feel desperate, but I don't want to push. I have always been desperate to get you back every time you have travelled away from me, even for an inch.

But now we are right next to each other, yet miles apart. I believe we will feel better soon. I just believe. Often it is all about belief, right? We believe in love, we believe in the romance that exists in books, we believe in tomorrow, we believe in the god(s). But then, in love, it is not just about belief. but trust. The kind of trust that blindly binds two people in everything.

Does this make sense? Not really, but that's how it is. Not everything makes sense in love. But when it does, it is so beautiful and pure. We talk, but we don't listen. We smile every day, but we don't laugh often. Something is missing, and all of it collectively comes together in our conscience as that one thing which we leave unnoticed, or take for granted, or treat with carelessness.

If we knew it, we wouldn't do it.

Someone is keeping it from us. And that someone is inside us.

I want us to realize this. I want us to realize us. Like the hundred times you have already done, can you trust me one more time? I don't know if it is the answer to our question, but I know it will matter. Conversations matter. Will you trust me? Do you trust me? Write back. I am listening.

***

SHE: (The right to remain silent)

It felt so odd, for me at least, to stay silent like this, without talking. I know we are writing letters to each other, and I am responding to you duly now. But still, it feels like a silent phase of slumber is overpowering me. I feel silence(d).

What is the use of silence? It heals. It hurts. Right now, the latter is more.

Either of us could have talked, but I didn't want to be the one who makes the move again. I am tired of that endurance. I don't want to sound harsh, but that's how I feel. I am totally disappointed with the way things have turned out. I do not know how we arrived here. I mean, look at us, living under the same roof, unable to find peace with each other after all these years of endless love.

I thought our love was an endless ocean of pleasant, positive surprises. You always surprised me with little things and silly gifts. I wouldn't have liked the gifts always, but I loved the surprises. It felt special. Remember the time when we fell in love with each other? We were the ideal couple amongst all of our friends. Everyone celebrated and envied us. They said we were made for each other. That we were crazy together.

Even in the most crowded places, you would always find space to embrace me in your warmth. It always made me feel like I had everything I could ever ask for. Where has all the warmth gone? I know I sound cliché. That's how I felt even when people debated over the love fading after marriage.

But right now, I am unable to rise past this cold distance between us. Maybe it is true, and it is only a matter of time before we get to realize it. Who are we? Where are we? I don't know if words will help me. Somehow, all I need is some silence. I want to be hurt, to take in that feeling and not just ignore it. Pain is comforting. I feel so now.

* * *

HE: (Do you hear me?)

Well, you have no idea how I feel either, in this state of mind. Do you know how it feels to be in a fight in love? It is like knowing the truth with clarity but fighting hard to speak it out. You fall short of words to explain how you feel inside, but manage to express it precisely. But I am full of words to explain how I feel inside, yet falling short of words.

The contradictions between us... You talk about how ideal we *were*. I still feel how ideal we *are*.

For instance, at my office today, when there was a conversation on how to enjoy freedom in a relationship, they took us as an example, given the way you had let me be on my own. They said it usually isn't so in a relationship, as there are changes after marriage, and that one has to confine themselves, confide and nothing else. You know how typical it gets during talks about such topics.

But it isn't in our case, I believe. You always let me be. I still feel I share the same warmth with you, no matter what. Maybe we are busy in our own worlds sometimes and I fail to express that at times. But it doesn't mean I don't love you. What is love, after all?

So much has been discussed about it already. It's pathetic to see how our instincts are being commoditized. Love, sex, compassion, and just everything that makes us human are a market commodity now. Remember when we used to read a lot of books, especially romantic novels, and dream of our soul mate in our own ways? Those were golden days.

You always wanted a tall guy, who kept his fingernails clean, knew how to make you laugh, could sing along with you the melodies of '80s, be able to carry himself and yourself well in any occasion, could dominate you once in a while, making your decisions easier, and harbour a love for travelling and opportunities to travel far to live life anew.

You had a very interesting set of expectations, or should I say fanatic dreams. I am not sure if I fit the bill, but definitely I can make good of a few of them, and I guess that's how dreams come true. It is like they don't happen all together at one go, but that spark to start with and everything else is lit in the course of time.

We talk about living the time we have in hand, but certain things are timeless, aren't they? Like these little things that are so nice to look back at. I can even hear your voice over the phone, telling me these dreams you had about your would-be soul mate. We weren't in a relationship then, but, we were friends who had each other's back all the time.

In a way, it was a golden phase when we were friends. We had no real pressure to persuade our parents for any commitment like marriage or no real sense of losing anything. I do miss that phase. Keeping apart the physical intimacy, what really is the difference between love and friendship? Some might call it a thin line, but I don't see a line.

When you love someone with all the might you have, care for the person sincerely, share the ups and downs always, and be there when they need you, isn't that special and mutual in both love and friendship? But I guess it is the craze or madness that makes the difference. It is hard to explain this feeling while in love, whereas in friendship it is so very easy to put out in words and deeds.

Does it ultimately boil down to the physical intimacy? Or is it something that transcends the physical emotions, both in love and friendship? Our basic instincts and pleasures often block our vision from getting a perspective of anything. In love, it is complicated. That urge to belong to each other, that irresistible instinct that guides us along the path, the magic that defies logic, that dawn of an understanding after a fight, that understanding without any explanation, that rare smile that you only gift to each other, that rage of confusion even in the easiest situations... sigh!

Love is quite a journey more than a destination. In fact, there never is a destination, there's only the path that takes the souls back and forth. It is not always forward, no! The direction is often backward, too, back into the memory lane where all the beautiful time spent together remains frozen. Years like months like weeks like days like hours like minutes like seconds like moments like... it all just goes so fast but memories are all we got.

More than the dreams, it is the memories that mean a lot. Nothing is as real as what had happened in the past. You were there, and did those things and felt some things. How intense is that? The power of memories to nurture dreams! It's hard to define a line that separates them in love.

In love, everything is timeless. I hear my voice when I write this. Do you hear me?

* * *

SHE: (What should we do?)

I hear you. I sincerely do. I wish I could help you, but don't know how to. Sorry for being rude, but like I said, silence is all that my mind seeks now. I don't know about the heart. Or perhaps our generation has romanticized it too much for selling films and greeting cards. Our feelings are a by-product of what we see, and what others see in us. The heart has nothing to do with how we feel, right? It is all up in the head.

Or perhaps it is when we fail to use the head that we put the blame on the heart. Someone has to take the blame, anyway. Nobody wants to own responsibilities, but own each other in the name of love. I am reminded of possessiveness – a celebrated word in the game of love. Usually, it is a raging phenomenon when two people fall in love.

The girl doesn't like the boy eyeing other girls, and the boy doesn't like the girl befriending other boys. It seems silly in hindsight but right then it would be a measurement of how much one loves the other. Slowly, as the days pass, it fades. And obviously, after marriage, other big things take the centre-stage and this possessiveness factor nearly disappears.

But ironically, in my case, it is just the opposite. I wasn't really that person who regulated your actions and friendships. Nor had I controlled you in any sense. But after marriage, it changed completely. I actually became possessive of you, for obvious reasons that you made me feel so.

In fact, if you remember (I am sure you do) I had told you once, "I am okay if you want to have a physical relationship with someone in your life after our marriage. I will happily allow you to give life to your instincts, just for once. Don't say no. I want you to experience a love beyond me, for once. But I can never bear to share you emotionally with any other person. Just don't fall in love with anyone emotionally, will you?"

I don't know how much sense it made, but I remember really meaning that. But within six months of our marriage, the same person who had posed such a liberal statement took it back, saying. "I am sorry, I can't. I don't know why I just can't accept such a thing ever. Just don't ask why!"

Why was I insecure? Of course, you were this person who never believed in marriage and the restrictions that it brought to a free spirit like you. I knew what I was getting into when I landed on your soul's door, which always remained open for me to enter and contemplate myself.

Never in my life had I felt like I belonged more, than when I was with you. I don't know how to put it across. I am not good with words like you are, but what has truth got to do with language or diction? I loved you truly, and every little movement towards you was both conscious and unconscious. I knew you were already in a relationship by then, and that you can never really stay committed to anything, much less a relationship.

You always wanted to be a free spirit. Your understanding of love is different from mine. I knew what I was getting into, when I held your hands for good. I have no regrets, but just the amassing uncertainties that I am struggling to cope with. You don't think too much or worry about life. I wish I could be like you. That would solve a lot of problems.

I accept my limitations.

I don't know if I am sorry. Even if so, I just don't want to accept it, and don't know how to. Every time I am lost and stranded, I end up coming to you for the answer. I am ready to listen. I am open to a conversation. Tell me again.

What should we do?

* * *

HE: (The Proposal)

I have no control over this trip that transcends us into another dimension. I am now reminded of the most important evening in our journey. Let me be honest, I don't remember the date. But I know the time. It was 6.30 PM; you had gotten down from your usual share-auto ride at the Adyar Depot signal after work. It was a busy street as always. You were wearing that blue Kurti with white pearl drops spread all over. But you weren't really yourself that day.

You had had a troubled day that had started with a series of hiccups at work. You also had a sore throat, along with confusions about priorities in life, plus the random chaos that the mind pulls in from all directions. That's a lot to feel together. Altogether you were down, I remember talking to you earlier that morning when you broke down over the phone owing to the kind of stress you were into.

I understood that you needed a shoulder to rest on. That is all it takes at times. Those days, I used to come to Chennai only when work called. But when I did, I made sure I spent the evenings with you and just walked along with you from the share auto drop stop to your hostel. It was a 2

KM route, and we used to talk so much during that walk.

Somehow that walk meant a lot. It assured and reassured, like rain and rainbow. It just was so. That evening was different though, under the summer sky. There was a difference in the way it spilled light. It was oddly beautiful. I was there, leaning on a lamppost that had a political party flag at its top. I was nowhere inclined to the party or its principle, but to the post, yes, for the moment.

A tree would have been much more soothing, but where is the space for green except in the dollar notes? And there you came, jumping out of the crowded auto. Right from that moment, you were silent. I respected that and kept walking along with you. We walked past the tender coconut shop, the Karaikudi Restaurant, and Optics showroom ahead. It was about to drizzle.

Usually, I would be mindful of the people walking by and life happening around us. But I wasn't intimidated then, for my attention was heaped towards your obviously disturbed mood. In our silence, I kept hearing a million words that mattered. We'd known each other for three years over endless conversations, but those few minutes of silence seemed to prove the most important things.

Just as we crossed the Adyar Anandha Bhavan restaurant, I strode a step faster than you, and came to your front left side. I had always let you be in the front, for I wanted to have your back. For the first time, I had taken the lead and before I knew, I held your hands and stalled. There was a peal of thunder that the universe had timed to this second. I heard it, you heard it, but WE didn't. Our physical hearing detected it but our souls were too loud to bother about something trivial as thunder.

You looked at me, perplexed. I looked at you, calm and poised. For a second, everything else faded and it was just you and me. I moved a little to my left so I could see both your eyes in front. They held an ocean of tears held back at the brim. I will never forget those magical words that I spelled even before I was consciously aware of them.

"Can we live this life together?"

You replied with tears that had struggled so hard to stay within the seam of your eyelids until then, demanding, "What took you so long to ask me this?"

I didn't ask you to marry me, and there was no cheese in the cake we had in our hand. I wanted you to live with me. You didn't say YES, but beyond that, you answered with a question. Right there, under the drizzle of your eyes and amidst the happening universe, we were destined to be.

There were a lot of factors surrounding the moment: the kind of chaos our relationship would evoke when we validate it socially, our families that would be startled, and so much more. I knew it all, and remarked, "Just think of you and me, and then our parents. Everything else is on me. I will stand tall to make sure we see the light!"

We didn't speak after that. We held hands, walked, and looked around unseeingly. We only felt the magic that was in the air. We both felt that the conversation that had happened was enough for a century. We reached the sharp left turn that led to the street beside your hostel. Once we reached your place, we did not stop. We turned and trailed back the way we came, like a tape roll wound back.

It was liberating. It felt like time travel. Somehow it felt like a huge burden off our chests even though there wasn't one in the first place. We started talking about things that grabbed our mind's attention. We talked about the first time we met, the last time we fought, the sunrises we'd seen together, the sunsets we'd missed like forever, the journeys we loved, the destination we had no clue about, the similarities we shared, the differences we loved...

The conversation went on as we walked the length and breadth of the entire Sasthri Nagar. There were petty shops that we crossed twice, and tailor shops that we crossed thrice. We didn't care about the gleeful glances that people gave us when we laughed out of our hearts. The most beautiful smile came from the lady stringing jasmine flowers for her evening sale. Somehow, that sealed the chaos and gave way to the harmony we had for the rest of the evening.

We didn't reach any conclusion but only talked and talked. It felt good and true. By the time we reached your hostel, we let go of our hands that had stayed glued all the while. The cool breeze of the air that kissed the palm brought about a coldness that made us realize the inch of gap we had. We held hands again, only to realize that this friction was the most beautiful pressure we had ever felt in this lifetime; one that gives peace and space.

I bid a reluctant goodbye to you. You smiled. Nothing else was needed, that smile of yours held my life in its lip. Sigh.

✳ ✳ ✳

SHE: (The walk to remember)

What can I say? That evening, that drizzle, the way we held our hands, that walk we had... everything remains etched as a nail hammered onto a tender tree. Those words you asked me, those eyes that pierced into me... everything remains so fresh. It is hard to explain how I felt at that time. But what I can say is how it feels to look back at that moment from here. It feels simultaneously real and magical.

Real, because it all started from there, and we are here together, talking about it. Never have I experienced that kind of intensity with anyone or even anything else in my life. It is with such strength that you struck me. It stays vibrantly alive, even this very second when I think of it. A second holding a minute? That's how I feel. You beautifully described it.

From my eyes, it felt even more beautiful and most importantly, painful. Because I knew you were in a relationship earlier, not for the sake of it but for 4 sincere years. I knew that meant a lot to you. So right from the moment I had known you, there were these instances when I would be grounded by reality, and a mind that fails to accept the fact that we hadn't met earlier in life.

What if we had known each other years ago? What if we had been friends from school? What if we had been souls that found love in college? What if we eventually realized that we were meant to be forever? What if we sang our favourite melodies together whenever the car's radio played it? What if we got to sleep in each other's arms and woke up breathing on each other's necks? What if we just stay together, like forever?

I use to have so many dreams, but keep them all to myself. Also, I knew in my heart that you are not the person who should be confined to a commitment, and you ought to be free and wild as you are. Marrying you was never my dream, but companionship was. Yet, every other factor in the external world pulled me back. I remained calm. You do not know how it feels.

That evening was no different for me. There were endless evenings earlier too, when I used to walk that 2 KM distance with these thoughts in my mind and superficial smiles on my face. I would miss you, and love you more. I would yearn for you, yet despise you. I would love yet hate you. It was like dying one second to being born the next second. So going through all this, when you asked me those magical words that evening, "Can we live this life together?" I was stabbed with a powerful sword of ecstasy.

A sudden wave of pain and agony passed through me and all I could do was look into your eyes and cry my heart out wordlessly. I have tears even now as I speak of the happiness I had when you held my hands then. Of everything we spoke in the while, the most meaningful words were those that our hands shared. The warmth and the sweat, it just happened to be the fuel, and the fluid of my senses. I cherished each and every second we spent walking to and fro.

Never had I held someone's hands with so much love and posterity. I was smiling all the way through. You didn't notice, for it was from the inside and very little was shown outside. It was too precious to be flaunted visibly. I am unable to bring any order to this feeling at all. How to prioritize it? The pain or pleasure? I guess they are one. We did know in each other's heart that we deserved to be together. But it took a scratch of light to come through, and call it life.

✻ ✻ ✻

HE: (Such certainty)

That sparks a million thoughts within me again, and I am trying to organize them. It is so hard for me to be organized. That is easily my biggest weakness. I am uncertain most of the time, and there is no plan. Let's take my love for writing. The only thing I am certain about is that I want to be a writer. But have I written a book? No. Do I maintain a blog? No. Do I have a list of poetry or prose collections to portray? No.

Then what is that air of confidence I have when I say I want to be a writer, as if I am already one in the making? If you ask me what writing means to me, I would say I flirt with every minute, cuddle every hour, make love to life every day, and eventually bear the child of the thoughts in my mind. I take time, gestate, and when its time, I just can't wait to deliver. I bleed through my fingers and give birth to words!

Now that's how my writing happens. For me, writing is not a passion or a profession or a calling... it is a way of living. It is a responsibility. I don't see myself doing anything other than writing. In such an intense form of expression. If I think of you, I am fascinated by the way you've always made me write. You excite me mentally. My favourite poems ever written have been for/because of you. You have always been my perennial source.

On a lot of instances, you had told me how you were overwhelmed by how my words depicted you, better than what you actually were. But let me tell you, it is from the source that the stream arises. And no matter what, the stream can never rise above its source, be it light or water or sound or emotions. You are my source, and I am your stream that flows through boundlessly.

Everything is a copy of a copy of a copy of a copy. The original creations are a matter of the heart when there is a connection between the universe and the self. You are a part of this magical connection, and naturally, everything else has fallen into place. You are a bridge that mattered and connected me with my own self. Maybe we are not always the same organic matter that decomposes. With enough love, we have our purpose redefined.

At the end of the day, we *are* special for that one soul that looks forward to us.

✳ ✳ ✳

SHE: (Fight is essential)

This fight is essential. Don't you think so? It has led to a series of events which otherwise are seldom discussed. How cruel is that? We have it all inside, but we don't have the time and space to express it. What stops us?

What breaks us? What makes us? I am reminded of what Tyler Durden says in the Fight Club movie,

"We're consumers. We are by-products of a lifestyle obsession. Murder, crime, poverty, these things don't concern me. What concerns me are celebrity magazines, television with 500 channels, and some guy's name on my underwear. Rogaine, Viagra, Olestra."

True, isn't it? I confess that I am in this circle of materials, partly. I feel guiltier because I know this, yet I do this. Most of us do, don't we? Can we ever be true to our conscience? Can we live a need-based life? Can we keep the plastic straw out of our juice glasses? We can, but we don't. Somehow we remain a product of the environment. I am talking a lot like you do, I think. There is a lot of you living in me. These are cues from the rainbow that I saw last night.

There have been days when I would look at a flying plane and bend till I lose balance. Now that I go by it, I can see only buildings and landscapes as tiny pieces. But a few things never change. There are spectators who still chase the plane. I just can't see the little children on the land, running and jumping, desperately trying to catch the plane. But I am sure they still exist. No harm in it.

Some dare to catch it someday, some dare to buy it someday... and some dare to pilot it someday. Someday... they would. That someday would not come until institutions train minds to think, rather than celebrate the school results topping the lists every year! This can't happen until politics die in colleges! Not until a student is rewarded for his originality rather than being punished for failing to follow the usual syllabus/procedures.

Schools, colleges, jobs, cricket, appointments, appraisals, hard work, success, failure... everything seems useless for a second. Everything is incomplete. Everything is right here, not hidden elsewhere. It's not something else. It's you and me 'which' are incomplete. The use of 'which' is applicable, for we are nothing but laughing social animals that still see women as a sex symbol on the screens, and chase money and call it the dream.

Like an art so clear, and an untold love so dear, things happen, and keep happening. A lot of what is scribbled here remains senseless to me, just like it may look to you; until really looked into, until really laughed for or at, and until really wept about. With so many things to worry about, tell me, will you believe me if I said that I saw a rainbow last night?

I mean where is the space for imagination when everything is an experience or a product price tagged and promoted as an emotion?

✷ ✷ ✷

HE: (The rainbow I saw last night?)

"The rainbow I saw last night!" – Ah, the world of memories attached to it! It was the title of the first article I ever wrote, and it revolved around my frustrations with the things that I saw around me. I was doing my MBA then, in Noida. For someone who doesn't know Hindi, to be in any part of the country other than one's home state is like surviving in a foreign land.

But this also allowed me the sense of freedom that a foreign land gives. At times, it is not inclusivity that gives you space, but being excluded that lets you be. I was alone and agile. I wrote against a lot of things in the system back then. Let us admit, we are not even allowed to kiss in our homes when there is family around, let alone kissing in public. Section 377 is cleared only on papers, but not in the minds of the people who are still irked when the same sex people get along in love, forgetting that love is an emotion of the soul.

Inter-caste marriages are still a sin in many places. Weekend sales are seen more importantly than blood donation campaigns. Our entire generation is canned to consumerism. Everything is tied to an outcome of commerce, like a beautifully packaged lie. Invariably, the way we relate to life, the way we live, the way we love are dependent on the way we submit ourselves to the system.

What change can we possibly bring about as an individual? But at least, can we trigger a conversation... Conversations are my addiction. That is how we found love in each other, too. The revelation of an idea in a conversation inspires me. Once revealed, it floats high and thrives bold. Ideas are bulletproof as V said. God, I am reminded of 'V for Vendetta' now. Remember all those powerful dialogues? Our lives were lit with such characters. Our understanding of each other was more through these characters in books and movies. They were our mutual friends. We hung out with them, and laughed and cried with them. We even became them. We weren't really worried about who we were on the outside but always cared about who we were on the inside.

What do we call this? Love? But why should love be the ultimatum all the time?

I'd call it 'resonance'. The way we resonated with each other formed the basis of our relationship. That connect that we had... how to name it? I don't want to call it 'love'. Sometimes it is more than love, the feeling when two souls resonate. It is more than a definition. It is a raging vibe. Energy doesn't lie. This is physics, and it has to be acknowledged. At the end of the day, such souls get together, no matter what, and send ripples of love into the universe that will become the twinkles that we see, in the stars up above the sky.

Chapter 3

The Train Of Memories

HE: (Our first phone call)

How did I even imagine something like the rainbow I saw last night? The title, I mean. When all the logic in the world fails, it is imagination that will help us stay alive. I believe in the power of imagination and its invincible nature. Like Einstein said, logic will take you from A to B. But imagination will take you anywhere.

I wanted to be that free spirit who could be anywhere, anytime. But that can be dangerous too. A kite without a thread can be anywhere, but it can end up nowhere too. But, is the destination important? Is it not the journey that counts? I don't know. You have to travel to find out.

I hope we can talk about our recent trip to Sri Lanka, and the way we stood lost in a lot of places. But my mind is still glued to 'the rainbow I saw last night'. Not because it became the most voted article on the Yahoo website it was featured in, or the most discussed article on the social forums where I shared, but because it got your attention.

Yes! Our very first conversation rooted from this article. A friend of my friend had shared it with you. You read it and messaged me, saying "I loved the rainbow you saw last night. Can you tell me more about it?"

That was how the text from an unknown number read. Before I could finish wondering who it was, you followed it up with a text saying, "I truly loved it!"

I smiled genuinely for a text message that was like a beam of sunlight. It was the first time a stranger read my words and reverted with curiosity to actually know more in person. You were not technically a stranger to me, for we had studied together in the same college for 4 long years, but we had seen each other just that once.

That was when you were attending a job interview, and I happened to go past you with my friend. You had grey contact lenses on that somehow seemed natural to me. We didn't talk much, apart from my cursory "all the very best". We didn't know then, that we will cross paths again, but there I was, smiling over your text message and feeling intrigued that you liked my words.

My words are very personal to me. Like they are a part of me, at least, expressed nakedly.

We texted a few times. And the next thing we knew, I had called you for a conversation that very night with no expectations but the need to explain the thoughts I had in my mind when I wrote that article. I called you around 9 PM. We talked. Strangely, there was no unfamiliarity between us talking for the first time.

We talked about the presence of politics in education, the absence of education in politics, the craze for celebrities, the cause of poverty, the cars on the road, the hole in the ozone layer, the love for books, the hate for caste discrimination, the peace of the birds on the trees, how the noise of the mobile networks disturbed the same, the importance of word count, the negligence of emotions in everyday life, what we see in the mirror, what happens when we talk to the stars, where can we find the meaning of life, the scent of books, the skin of movies, the music in wounds, the language of scars, the strange friends, the friendly strangers, openness of the universe, the closed wifi networks, serious grudges, casual sex, comfortable quilts, danger in mineral water bottles, fragrance of the flowers, importance of leaves...

It just went on and on. The only interruption was our mobiles flashing a low battery warning, and we had to take positions to get them charged. I felt the heat, for I didn't have a earphone to plug in and stay away from the charging phone. But nothing stopped us, and by the time the realization dawned upon us that we had been talking for 8 hours straight, the day dawned outside as well, with the birds chirping, and the clock ticking six.

Only in hindsight, a day later, did we realize that we had talked so much but not a word about each other, literally. I didn't get to ask anything about whom/what you were, the food you loved or the colours you sported, or the kind of music you liked. And you didn't ask me anything personal, either. It was a flow of thoughts and ideas about everything we laid our minds upon.

It was like the universe talked to itself, and we were its medium. It was a different kind of high that only a genuine conversation can evoke. More than speaking to each other, we enjoyed listening to the other. It felt like receiving a letter, every time we took turns and listened. After all the hours, and the endless conversations, the most beautiful parts were those final few minutes when we didn't have much to speak.

By then, we both were lit by the fact that we shared so many beautiful differences. It wasn't about feeling similar, no! It was about how we were able to accept each other and our differences as traits of our being. The level of acceptance we had was so bright that we could feel each other smiling in silence at each other, miles across, in two poles of the country. For the first time ever, I wanted to spell out those magical words the way they came out. I had it at my throat, and I am sure you had it on your tongue.

What stopped us? Of course, the fact that I was into a relationship then, and to express out loud that I loved someone from my heart for what they are, somehow was forbidden as a result of the social conditioning. You can't say so, when you are committed to someone for life. You just don't have the courage to be true to someone you just spoke with over the phone, however true it was.

There was no one else listening but us. So what made me hesitate? After all the contemplations I had over life, and the rage I had to challenge norms, I still wasn't able to say what I meant by my heart. In that microsecond, I said to myself, what am I ranting about when I say I would be making changes in the society, if I am not able to express even the most genuine emotion I hold inside right now?

I wasn't going to say anything out of lust or the natural laws of attraction, but only of the sheer goodness that I experienced after a heartfelt conversation. With all the courage and the character, did I spell it out or not? You knew it. I knew it. But it didn't matter. What mattered is the silence that prevailed for a few minutes that seemed like a long hour, and the way we heard each other out concisely. That was magic.

I saw you smiling then. I am smiling now, too. Can you see me?

✳ ✳ ✳

SHE: (Our first meeting)

You and your words, what is it between you both? Clearly I can't differentiate between them for it is one single emotion that I held in me when I read your words. I fall for your words every time I read them. Does that mean I was falling for you, as a person? As you said, your words are the most intense form of you, and I was falling in love with them.

I don't know. I think I did fall for you even without my knowledge or permission, somewhere down the lane. I didn't accept that, though, until you held my hands and looked into my eyes on that drizzling evening, years later. But it's too early to get to that moment now. There is so much more to reminisce.

I respected the fact that you were into a relationship then, and may be that by itself, brought on a screen of sense that stopped me from being vulnerable. More than love, I respected you. I admired you. A sincere wave of both these would come and garland my conscience whenever I was with you or speaking to you.

There were no boundaries between us, but we drew a circle around us that felt complete. We were happy to touch each other only on the outline that was lit enough already. We did not need to be one, we were happy as two circles who enjoyed being full and fat.

I am reminded of the first time I actually saw you for real, consciously. After around 2 years of talking over the phone and texts, one fine morning I was returning to Chennai after a weekend spent at home. My bus was to land in the city early that morning, and all of a sudden you had texted me, 'Let me come and pick you up in the morning. I will drop you to your PG'.

Woah, I didn't expect that! To me, you were an inspiration, a phenomenon, a passion, and a purpose. I didn't call you my friend, or lover, or anything mortally tangible. I saw you as my teacher, who had helped me realize who I was, constantly... and the one who made me believe in my character and charisma.

Yes, I felt beautiful when you were in my thoughts. Never have I felt so wholesome otherwise, rather than seeing beauty as something external masked in the layers of lipstick and face packs or the natural fair skin tone that was advertised as the standard of beauty by the industry. I always had this complex that I was dark skinned, but you chucked that silliness out of me, and made me realize how beautiful I am within the dusky duets of myself and my ego.

God, I can't explain how nervous I was, to even think of meeting you in person. Somehow I felt I didn't want to meet you at all. Yes, I was happily living a life with you in my mind; a dream that belonged only to me. What if it was disturbed by reality? What if the gravity of seeing you pulled down the butterflies I had in my head? I didn't want to lose any of the magic that thrived then, but I couldn't resist seeing you either.

It was you. What more can I ask for? But I didn't ask for that. I was perplexed. I was sleepless that night. The next thing I knew, I woke up to a horn that signalled my stop. I let my friends go on their way, and waited under that pole on Guindy Street.

'I am on my way.'

You had texted, a minute ago, and I was reading it hazily. Every slowing vehicle quickened my heartbeat. My heart was pounding. I wasn't able to control anything, let alone my heartbeat. I was looking at every corner, searching for you. And like the most natural thing I had ever seen, you rode up on your bike and stopped in front of me.

You were wearing a black helmet. Opening the visor, you gestured for me to hop on. I really didn't see your face properly. I was still in a blurry state of mind, and we were on our way to my hostel already. Someone I loved and respected so much, someone with whom I had shared endless conversations, someone with whom I had realized so many things about life and love and purpose, someone whom I looked upon for anything and everything...

That someone was right in front of me, or I should say, I was sitting behind him. Either way, we were together for the first time, and we didn't get to see each other or even speak a word properly! It didn't hit me until then, but we hadn't shared a word since we had met in person. But it didn't bother me. It just didn't matter at all.

For the first time in my life, I felt the magic of a physical presence. The mere presence of the soul that meant a lot to me made me feel at ease.

I wasn't tense anymore. My heart was beating fine. I didn't have any inhibition about talking to you, but I didn't feel the need to, either. It was perfect, the silence we had in the midst of the buzzing road that was alive with traffic.

I was smiling all the way, a part of it reflected in the shine of the black helmet. It was an old one, I suppose, but the shine was intact. I slipped into all the memories I held with you, and before I could cross an inch of its mile, my hostel came. You stopped. We stopped. But I didn't, I couldn't. I was still in motion as I got down and stood in front of you.

"Go and rest. We'll see each other soon again," you said with a smile, I faintly remember. Again, euphoria set in as you drove past, knocking the visor back in place. There I was, standing with a grin inside. On the surface, I don't really know how I was. I walked inside, with the smile that failed to fade. Everything else around me did, and it was just you and me in my mind.

It was only when I crossed past the first floor's window that I got to see my reflection, reassuring myself about the open smile I had on my face too. Before I reached my room, your texts came.

"I don't really know how to name this feeling. It is both serendipity and stupidity. I can't believe we didn't see each other properly or talk to each other at all. Yet, it felt liberating, as if we had opened up about everything we wanted to say. How can silence be so communicative? How can our souls be so complementing?"

"I don't know how you felt, but I trust that you felt that same way. I felt your presence. I felt comfortable. With you around, I didn't feel the need to express, or impress, or convince. It just was okay to be in my own world, yet feel the weight of togetherness. What are you?"

"You are a gift. Thank you for happening in my life. Keep happening!"

I was crying already, and I didn't stop. Rare are those moments we cry a lot out of happiness. I wasn't going to let a tear remain hidden. I love crying for both sadness and happiness. It makes me feel powerful. Sigh, one goddamn memory that I can't get over.

I want to live it all over again. Someday, sometime, soon!

✳ ✳ ✳

HE: (Dear Priya)

Why do, both the evening I proposed, and the morning we met for the first time, feel the same? Is it the intensity? Or the innocence? It is hard to explain. They are years apart, but still feel like the consecutive first and second pages of a book. I feel like the reader, and book that is being read, simultaneously.

The moment in hand now is somehow not about us, but by us. Do you understand the collective sense of individualism imbibed in this? I don't expect an answer, but love the certainty in these questions. In a world ruled by questions and answers, I feel that an abstract conversation is more important than anything else.

Like, what happens when we talk to the trees? How lovely it is to talk to the stars? When was the last time we kissed our legs? All of these might sound silly and stupid, but are essential, and connected. I am sure you are on the same page as I am, on this. Remember those nights you laughed out loud at me when I used to go to the terrace and talk to the stars? You have literally been by my side and laughed at my attempts.

But eventually, you did try once. You did talk to the stars. You didn't try it after that night ever, but I bet you felt that magic in the air. You either felt scared of such potent magic, or decided to let only one person out of us two stay crazy. Some stability is necessary.

What will I ever do without you? It is not just about the way you organize my backpack every time I head out on a trip, but more importantly about the way you look into my eyes every time I leave home. My home is not a concrete building, but the chaotic you. Every time I walk away from you, for whatever reason, you have that look in your eyes that pierces through my soul and reminds me of the way I felt when we took our first bike ride together.

The sheer warmth of the presence, and the sharp coldness of the absence, both hit me simultaneously. I find it hard to nod to one side. At times, I accept both sides. At other times, I ignore both sides. Never have I chosen one. Falter or fly high, it has always been a wholehearted approach I take when it comes to you.

Nothing ever about you has had a second thought. Such certainty... where do I get it? I mean, with every other thing in my life, I have always been uncertain. Where did I get this certainty of choosing you over anything and anyone else?

I am reminded of my first love, Priya, now. Let me share what I had written to her. This is yet to be posted, for I don't know her address yet.

Dear Priya,

I am 30 years old, married to the universe, and (in?) a passionate job that keeps me obsessed about todays and tomorrows. Life, at any given point of time, looks so hazy and busy, but in its entire blur, lies vivid the special memory of the first time I saw you.

1991, 2nd standard section A, Eden Gardens school, Salem. It was a Monday morning, the kind that bore the sadness of a disappeared weekend. I lived close to the school, and was early. As always, I was sitting on the first bench and watching the fellow students entering one after the other. The old Ayah Mas were cleaning the floor. With that sound of the bristles rubbing on the earth, a cloud of dust rose from the ground that was lit by the fresh sunlight.

Just when it seemed like yet-another-Monday morning, cutting through the haze and calling upon the grace, entered this new girl I had never seen before. It was you. You owned the next hundred seconds of my life totally. You were wearing a yellow t-shirt and a black skirt that had small yellow flowers printed all over.

Everyone was talking about you already, as they do when a new student arrives. But I was in silence, taken aback by the kind of feelings that were running inside me. There was a strange buzz inside. Too early to speak about love, but it was a beautiful feeling. I wasn't able to comprehend it.

Latha Miss came in shortly to take her class. As the ritual had it, any new comer was to come forward to introduce themselves to the class. You stood up and with a few gentle steps came to the front of the class, turned around and said, "My name is Priya. I am from Salem. My father is a manager in Canara Bank. My mother is a housewife. I love singing. Mahatma Gandhi is my role model. I will work hard and will become the President of India one day".

That was one flow of words and thoughts.

"That's brilliant Priya. Well said. Everyone, clap your hands for Priya... And let's welcome her to our school," said Latha miss.

I hadn't heard anyone speak with such grit and confidence till then. All of us clapped and mine was the loudest. I can still hear the thud sounds fading into one ball of realization that I had grown fond of you by then. From then on, you became one of the happy reasons for me to come to school. You had this habit of smilingly wishing a good morning to everyone in the class as you entered in the morning.

The smile would touch random people in its glance, and when it did reach me, I would be confused and perplexed. You had a dense smile. It held the depth of the colour green, and brought a fresh wave of life into me.

Somehow in the class you were the only person I didn't speak to often. I was comfortable looking at you from far, with two rows and seven columns of benches between us. Distance is bliss. It gives you the courage and the freedom to view something you love the way it is. Proximity brings familiarity and that might breed contempt.

The awe lies in the unknown. What if you come and talk to me? What if I stumble while speaking back to you? What will I say to you? What if you are fond of me like I was of you? What if we become best friends and stay friends forever? These 'what ifs' were more powerful than what really happened. And we did get to stand closer to each other when he monitored the class.

Remember, we had separate class leaders for boys and girls then. I was heading the boys, and you headed the girls, being the first rank holders in our respective genders. We would stand in the same line, few meters apart, and look at the class in front.

"Hey, boy!"

That's how you called me for the first time, and always after that, too. The 'hey' felt like 'hay' and the 'boy' felt like wind. It came together, the feeling of a breeze on a sunny afternoon, every time you called me. It would mostly be to ask something about the classes or homework you missed in your absence.

We had a friendship going, and I liked it. It felt good. All of a sudden I got used to liking the thought of you. I was neither an adolescent to feel the high of a physical attraction, nor a child who doesn't know the difference between fire and water. This was different. I hadn't watched many movies then, so I had no idea what love led to. I hadn't read stories then, so I had no clue about what to make of such a lovely feeling.

All I knew was that I liked you, and your presence meant something positive. I did not know what to make of it. I just loved it. Let me confess that your dense smile is one of my oldest memories of us, and I could still feel it. I can still see you with that thick curve on your cheek when you smile.

In the high of this, I unavoidably got transferred to another school. You have no idea how much I missed you. Especially since I had not shared this feeling with anyone else, it was real tough to cope. Thanks to the innocence of a third grade student, I did get past it, only until I saw you once again on the streets accidentally a year later. I was going in an auto-rickshaw to school when you were there walking on the left side of the street. I looked at you and was stunned into silence.

There is a mood to every phase of life. When we think of the past, when we think of ourselves at various ages, it comes with a mood that is almost tangible but floating in the air unseen, like music or the climate. That day when I saw you after a long time stands as a season by itself, one where the trees are full of leaves and life. They call it spring, right? We don't have it here, for all we have is winter or summer or rains.

But it was spring for me either way, especially when you had seen me, too. As I stood still, you had noticed me and called out, "Hey boy!"

That was all you said, and every echo of it remains etched inside me still. Before I could take my eyes off you, we sped past. I kept looking at you for as long as I could, sticking my neck out of the auto's perimeter. You stood still, too. You could've moved, but you didn't. That was special. In a way, it made me believe for the first time that you could've held back for me.

You could have stopped, because that was your stop, but to me it felt like you were conscious about what you were doing. Movement is natural, but a pause is intentional. Seeing you standing there with a fixed look at me moved me. Slowly and steadily, we got blurred, and that was the last time I saw you. In a way I let go of you, but in another way, I secretly seeded you deep into me.

I don't know where to post it. It doesn't matter, either. I'm sure you would have thought of me somewhere someday. I wish to believe so. This is true. My love for you was true. We will always be the boy and girl we knew, all so new.

Yours lovingly,

Prem boy.

✳ ✳ ✳

SHE: (Possessiveness?!)

What a beautiful feeling it is to have a crush? It is altogether a different world. I wish I had written letters to my crushes too. I had many but took only a few of them sincerely, though I always kept it to myself. There is no reciprocation in the world of crushes. Like an unsent letter, it was as idiotic and intense. Honestly, it wasn't a surprise for me, reading this letter. Not because you had told me about Priya already, but because I had read this very letter before.

You had kept this in your trunk case on the shelf. Naturally, as the one who keeps things in order at home, I happened to clean your shelf and hence the accident. Okay, it wasn't an accident exactly. I did peek into the box purposefully. And of everything, this letter caught my fancy. I was smiling all through reading it. As much as I cherish experiencing life with you in the present, I have always missed the times when we were not together. Any glimpse to your past lit me up, and I would submit myself to the moment.

It was strange yet special, to feel happy about reading your love letter to someone else. Was I comfortable because it was only a memory that you fantasized and wrote about? Or was I in love with you enough to accept the fact that you had loved someone else? I don't know. Somehow it has always been a testing ground, the way I am to accept your friendship with any girl other than me.

I mean, I know it is all fine and good to be closely connected to any soul that resonates, but why is it hard when it comes to you alone? I wouldn't call it possessiveness. But the time that they had stolen away from me - that's why it disturbs me when I see you close with anybody. I yearn for you every second, and still feel I couldn't get enough of you.

I was not the kind of person who thinks about one person all the time. I was like you, too. I had my own share of stories with people and things. I was like that even when we were in a relationship. But the moment we married each other into our lives, everything changed. I am not talking about the actual thaali you tied to me, and the one I tied to you. No. Neither of us wears it anymore.

It is about that moment when we started living together for good. Somehow, it struck me as an exhilarating blow that I never expected. I took you in wholly, and made you my life. I know it is stupid to lose my sense of self, but that's how it happened. I had no control over this. I started seeing you in a crazy way that I couldn't comprehend.

As days passed, it only got worse. I'm supposed to say that it was for better, but I spelled the word worse. It is true, for I know I was becoming something that I am not. I have no regrets, though. Just that I find it hard to battle a strange kind of possessiveness.

It is not that they crossed the barriers or there was anything unnatural about it, but they were so real and intense for me to get through. I wasn't able to share any part of your mind beyond myself. How selfish is that? But how lovely is that?

***

HE: (Going with the Flow)

I know this feeling, not by myself, but from the tears you've tried to hide when we have fights about me conversing closely with other souls. I wouldn't call it possessiveness, for we never wanted to possess each other. You can't try to own someone and call it love. It might feel sweet righteously then, but it is just not right.

Love is freedom. Love is when you feel winged enough to fly, yet remain rooted. It is not only about falling, but also rising together to reach heights that matter. Love is about inspiring each other to be better beings rather than two individuals confined to each other's world. Life is not as short as it is said to be. It is as long as art, given the way we paint it, listen to it, taste it and live it.

But given all this mutual understanding, why did it hurt you when I was emotionally connected to somebody else? I don't ask this to you, but to myself. We've had multiple fights over the same, yet, I've always given you more options to feel frustrated every now and then. Is it because I don't respect your feelings? Or do I love these attractions of the heart? Or is it my submission to a new vibe?

You've asked me these questions already. And my answers have always been heard. But ultimately, it is the love you have for me that brings an understanding that gives us peace and lets us move on. It is so hard to explain one's nature. I am a soul who loves to connect and contemplate. It somehow makes me what I am, always receptive to thoughts, ideas, and people.

I don't know how to forbid it, for I am myself when I am open to the universe that keeps playing games. I am happy to be the victim, vulnerable and vindictive. In a way, that's how I write, too, by making love to life and getting pregnant with the thoughts. Ultimately, there comes a time when I give birth to the children through my fingers onto the paper. And it takes this pain and freedom to give birth to genuine, original, words.

There are layers of myself that I don't understand or even try to. I let myself be so I can thrive to be a better version every day. It is hard to confine myself to anything other than you. I am a free spirit, as my MBA professor Ashwin Bhatia called me back then. I will never forget that midnight walk I had with him a day before I left Noida after finishing my masters. Somehow he was the first soul who said I 'needed' to write.

"No matter what you do, be it business, or branding, or a marketing job, I want you to write. That's what you're meant for. Your purpose lies in writing. It can be a blog or a book or for a magazine… just write. You need to… you have to," he said, as we crossed that park bench in Sector 110

The pizza we ordered also came by. It was past 12.30 AM, and we were having a walk that had been planned for months. His wife Anjali and two little angel daughters were sleeping at home, giving him the space to be. We communicated a lot, about love, family, friendship and companionship. We munched on the farmhouse pizza in our hands. It was the happiest pizza I ever had.

He means so much to me, and always calls me a free spirit. I felt the truth when he said that... May be I am a spirit that cannot be contained. No soul should be, for that matter. And my mental excitation was from conversations that I had with like-minded souls. It has always been so, and you know that. Our relationship was one such connection that stood its trials and saw the light, nothing less nothing more.

You were not just my excitement, but also my enigma. Everything else enters me, but you were there inside already. Like blood and water, thick and thin, we were together in a different way. I don't know how to put it. No stream rises higher than its source. You are my source, and my love, however large, is only a stream. I go with the flow.

* * *

SHE: (Love as it IS)

You and your words, again.

Though I can't accept everything you said, I still love it. I love the difference and your opinions. I am able to accept the essence but it still hurts, why is that so? Just my thing, and you wouldn't know it, for I have never placed you in such a situation. Like texting a poem to someone you admire – one that revolves around the difference of the breath's warmth in love and lust. It is fascinating to read, but why does it hurt when you share it with someone else?

Am I not supposed to love the life in a poem, the way I love you? Why do I expect to own it? I immediately put you in my shoes and imagine how you would react if I were so open and connected to love towards souls other than you. I want to, and see how you'd react... But I don't know if I ever can. I just don't seek anyone else.

Is it my fault? Should I be out there exploring life and love? Should I love myself more than I do you? After all, self-love is the best form of love, any day. You have always wanted me to be free. But my freedom lies in the circle I've drawn around myself. It has been a revolution to hold these thoughts of sharing you with anyone else, even if it meant for the slightest time or memory.

It hurts. It hurts hard. I don't shy away from expressing the pain I've endured, but that doesn't stop me from loving you. Is this a blessing or a curse? Am I right or wrong? The struggle is in trying not to seek an answer, for I already know it. The fight is to accept it and smile from the inside. I am fine with the pain, and this fight. I will go on to love us, as I always do.

To me, there is nothing more important than giving myself to you.

We all have our passion, and we keep pursuing our dreams to find our passion. Somehow all these things: my dream, passion, purpose... they all seem to be you. I am so convinced about this. I know I am the love of your life. I am happy if the distractions motivate you. I am happy if you talk to another soul that lights you up. So be it.

I hate to say this after all the feuds, but I love the way you stay open to life as it comes, going with the flow. I hope I can be like you someday, and experience love as it is, unbounded. But I don't need to, for that's not my search. I can't, for that's not my nature. I am happy with you.

✳ ✳ ✳

HE: (Scheme of love)

I hear you. I envy you.

You told me you wanted to put me in your shoes sometime and make me experience what you feel. I am not sure if I'd understand you as much as you do me. I love how you fight me every time, not to disassociate but only to understand each other more and get closer.

How much can we know about ourselves if we've never fought with each other? Scars are important. They remind us of realizations that nothing else can evoke. I've witnessed your transformation more closely than you did. My first memory of you is as a girl who only cared about the colour of her lipstick. You were this dashing diva who flaunts latest trends. You had an accent that I found funny, yet attractive.

Remember those early morning conversations we used to have by the seashore? We always used to go before dawn broke, and sit under the shade of the surreal pink skies. We would keep talking, and at times just revel in the silence of each other. We wouldn't be looking at each other but away into the horizon, lost and merged in a different kind of pleasure. Looking into each other's eyes didn't matter but looking onto the universe together did.

And just when the Sun and splashed its first rays of light, I would look at your side. You would still be seeing the waves. I have never seen anything more magnificent than the first splash of sunrise on your dusky skin. It is a revelation. A lot like our wet kiss on the terrace, this warm moment by the seashore stays in my mind. Sun and the moon, the source and the reflection, you and me, it just comes together, and apart simultaneously.

After letting the sunshine kiss us, we'd stand up and walk towards the Murugan Idli Shop for breakfast. Even in a traditional south Indian restaurant, your ordering style would be modern. I stayed the same silly me, who doesn't care about manners or habits. Indulgence was my thing, and I never missed a chance to slurp the sambhar out of my fingers, while you'd never have a stain on your finger despite eating with bare hands.

You can't eat Dosas with spoon, can you? But still, your fingers would look like you did. I'm trying to realize how different we were. But somehow I've stayed the same. But you've changed. For good or bad, I don't know. In fact, it wasn't about good or bad. Change is inevitable, but the extent to which you did surprised me.

You spoke about how I stayed open to love and relationships beyond commitment and marriage. I agree that I am open to express the love I have for another soul, any day; any time. You also expressed your desire to experience love like I did. What if I say that I wished the same too, that I would someday want to experience love the way you do – to be madly in love with a soul and set everything else free?

One soul loving more than one soul often raises eyebrows in the society. Most people are offended or startled. But a set of people also consider this to be forward thinking and contemporary. The one who is able to share love with more than one soul is liberal and elite. Are you getting what I'm saying? In another world of mere scientific terms, polygamy is considered liberal and monogamy is considered conservative.

But guess what? Years of research on this topic says just the opposite. They say it is normal to be attracted to like-minded souls. It is normal to be able to love everyone. There is nothing special in giving life to your instincts, that's basic. That's how we are, and we will be.

What is special is when you are so much in love with a soul that you rise above your basic instincts, resist your temptations for that soul which matters, kindle a new wave of desires just for that soul, spend time to understand, accept, give, take, stalk, surrender, submit, fall and rise in love just for that soul.

It is not easy to love a soul and stay committed to it for a lifetime. The commitment is not a choice taken, but a change that happens over time, unconditionally. I am not talking about the socially bound feeling that comes with a marriage, like the way married couples in India are advised and expected to stay married forever. That's a different topic altogether.

I am talking about the sense of certainty that arises when you are able to feel everything you need in one soul. A question arises, 'Is it the one who loves or the one who is being loved? Who is the luckier one of the two?' Blessed are the ones who reciprocate this magical feeling. Gifted are the ones who are in it, even without reciprocation. I feel gifted and blessed, too.

Marriages of souls that happen at this level of understanding are to be considered enchanted, contemporary, and classic. Everything else is natural. We've always fantasized multiple loves at any given point of time, and that we should never confine ourselves to the cage of commitment, but instead explore life and self limitlessly. I stay true to the same, but you changed.

Like a metamorphosis of self, you went through the pain of time and the pleasure of space, to become a butterfly that flutters with all its fragility into the universe, with nothing but love that has its roots in me. Is there anything stronger than the fragile wings of this butterfly?

* * *

SHE: (I love everything I hate you for)

Nature is beautiful. I've enjoyed our sunrise mornings the most, and in fact, every time the sun rose above the sea, it'd feel like the Sun had asked me out. It'd flirt with its rays and touch me with its warmth. I had every option to stand up and walk towards it until the waves hit my toes.

But I held my earth. I chose to stay by your side, and you'd drag me into the sea waves, right after this. Did you hear my words inside? What else was it? It is surreal that even in a dark room, I'd feel the same warmth and moisture of the sunrise by the beachside, when I'm with you. You are my sunshine; you are my seashore. There is nothing poetic in what I just said, just ordinary feelings finding its place on this letter.

Is it ok to be ordinary? In this world of benchmarks and product reviews, it is hard to be original, especially if it means being ordinary. There is nothing wrong with that, though. Why does everything need to be interesting and impressive all the time? We have to accept that we are all tired of impressing each other. Real freedom when there is no more need to convince anybody but yourself.

Again, I feel like I am speaking a lot like you. This is not myself. I don't give a damn about anything beyond a peaceful day and unperturbed sleep in the night. I feel new now, and I am liking it. May be I am the butterfly from the silk moth that escaped the phase of being killed for the silk in it. Honestly no one has the time, either for the silk to happen naturally albeit a bit slower, or for the food that is best felt when cooked by hands rather than one that is delivered.

Too many situations to select from, and so many prepositions to connect with. It certainly is so hard to achieve these days, even on Netflix. Too many options to browse, making us doubt our verdict. It is so everywhere today. Enter into a supermarket; you are filled with the sight of endless shelves of various products. I am that confused consumer in line, wondering and pondering into the colourful imagery and feeling good about purchases I'd later second guess.

I might be the one who plans it all in our life, but I concede I was not good at it. When being something is the only choice you have, you will become the person that it takes to be. But I have my set of commotions, especially bewilderment, every now and then.

I feel like I need help. I get frustrated that you haven't yet taken up more responsibilities. Your wayward living pushes me to the edge so often. It's like a maze. We are all our own kinds of mazes, aren't we? Mazes we built around ourselves, and end up complaining about, too.

Nothing is certain, but you.

I know the flaws that you come with, the chaos that you are, the series of unpredictable events that you are made up of, and the recklessness that you exhibit. But nothing has stopped me from loving you the way I do. Why do I love you so much? Why am I so certain about you? I don't really know. It's like trying to remember something that never happened.

Ever since I knew you, I have always had this irresistible urge to love you. It only got better with time, like all matters of the heart. It is not about me loving you intensely, but how you brought out such awe from me. Twice or thrice, I have tried to decode this magic inside, but every time I was left with the same questions and no answers.

It took some time for me to understand that not all questions need answers. Especially in love, it just is so. No explanations or science should be involved in the matter of hearts; only the flow of moments leading to the next one. My love for you is an intoxication that no drug can bring, to this night that never ends.

I took time to understand this madness a little deeper, and I came to a realization that it is not only the way you love me that attracted me to you, but the way you love life at large. I loved your openness and how vulnerable you were. Never did I think that I would be sharing a conversation or space with a soul like you.

I have ample respect for your volatility. I love the fact that you are able to connect, transmit, and be receptive at the same time. I love the way you stay undisturbed by the worldly elements of materialism. I love the way you love souls. I love the way you accept souls.

I love everything I hate you for, too.

✳ ✳ ✳

HE: (Railing thoughts)

Love and hate, two contradicting things that hold each other. You do remember the conversation we had about certainty, don't you? We were sitting in the railway station, waiting for the train to arrive. Railway stations are magical, in the sense of how they become this dream junction for people coming together to board for their destinations. Everyone is on their way towards something, with a world of thoughts in their heads. We had ours.

"What is it about this humid air that is there in Chennai railway stations?"

"Come on, thousands of people put together, plus the warmed up engines, the heated arguments, and the Chennai climate. That's a lot of heat to handle, even for M. S. Dhoni."

"Ironically, he did start his life here, didn't he? As a ticket collector. Do you think this place has anything to do with his life today?"

"Of course! Everything is connected to something. The way you do something will be the way you do everything. Cricket was his passion. What inspires all of us more than it, is the person that he is. Don't you agree?"

"I am not much of a cricket fan, but I do like MSD's temperament. The only true player I really cheered for, was Suresh Raina, and that other bowler in CSK. What's his name? Everyone chanted it when we watched a live game! Aargh! I am not able to recollect. I've told you right? Some Molly or something..."

"It's Bollinger,"

"Yes! Bollinger! We chanted along when CSK took on RCB. I had no idea who he was, but it was fun to chant with the crowd."

"More like the reason we take up Engineering. I mean, I had no clue about anything when I took up the Electrical and Electronics Engineering course, except for the fact that my father was an Electrical Engineer, and he did well in life. I thought I could become one, too. But I got it all wrong. I wish I had had the firmness to choose what I wanted to study back then. A lot would've been different by now."

"We are prone to go with the flow. As much as it sounds like magic and in sync with what the universe has planned for us, don't you think we need to take control too, at times? Like calling it quits or starting afresh at any point of life?"

"Yes indeed. If you ask me, we have to die inside at the end of every day. Only then can you be born anew the next day to take on life. Every day is a new life, and you are a different person. That's how it was, at least to me. I am talking about the kind of submission you need to make to the present, not carrying the past, or envisioning the future. Planning ruins the magic. Life has to be spontaneous, immense, and intense. What is anything other than this?"

"Reality. Anything other than this is reality."

"What is reality?"

"Who cares?"

"That's the point. Should we care or not?"

"I think we have to, in this sane world."

"We don't have an option actually. No matter how free spirited you are, you just can't say no to gravity can you?"

"Gravity is not responsible for people falling in love. How real is this quote?"

"So absurd. I'd say levitation is naturally possible for people falling in love. Do I win?"

"Aww, I happily lose to you."

"Certainly?"

"Certainly!"

"Ah! Come on, give me your hands. Let us just hold on to each other until our train arrives."

"We have 30 minutes left for that."

"I am glad you don't sweat in your palms. I know you have a rough palm – it runs in your family, you've said. Somehow I hate sweaty palms. I am just glad you don't have one."

"Good to know that."

"That's a lot of certainty for one evening, or night, to speak of!"

"Doesn't matter what the time says. What matters is the space that we are in. It moves doesn't it, this moment? Though we are grounded."

"What to do with this crazy head of yours that thinks like a poet?"

"I don't know. You know why I love train stations and train journeys? There are delays or cancellations, but by large, it is a junction of so many souls boarding huge machines, to reach their respective destinations. And they do land where they want to, eventually. In that brief while, so many words travel together in compartments that keep moving. Every person is a world unto themselves. Imagine so many worlds sitting in their allocated seats, calm and composed. When was the last time you saw such order and discipline in mass? Beautiful!"

"Discipline is beautiful?"

"You disagree?"

"No, I am just surprised that you are stating that. You don't even clip your fingernails or keep the socks in their place. Let alone the bigger things!"

"You don't have to be a role model or even a follower to speak out for what's true and beautiful. You don't have to be a poet to enjoy the sunrise. Yes, I do envy those who are disciplined and responsible. They just get things done easily, don't they? It is not the dreams anymore, but the execution, which is the new sexy."

"You've got to do what you've got to do."

"Now ask me something, will you?"

"Like?"

"Just ask me whatever you want to ask me. As simple as that. I suddenly feel like I need to answer some question of yours. Help my instinct!"

"How certain are you about us?"

"I don't want to discuss love now. But let me talk about us and the way we feel when we are together. There are times we travelled together for hours together, like that once when you came all the way to Salem to just drop me, took an immediate train back to Chennai and reached the very same night. That was dramatic.

"It was natural to board the train with an open ticket and pay to the TTR for a proper seat in the sleeper compartment. But we realized that you were cashless that day, that too only after you were on the moving train already. I was running alongside, to give you everything I had in my purse before the train fled off.

"You did get a seat and landed safe the next morning. It was a sleepless night for me, not because of anxiety, but because of what you did to me. Long after you were gone, I was sitting in the station and experiencing the space that you were in, merely minutes ago. It became an hour soon, and I suddenly fell in love with the station that I had frequented ever since I was a child. But this time it was different. We barely had 10 minutes to run, from the moment we bought the ticket, to the moment you boarded the moving train. I texted you then, saying how beautiful it would've been if you had missed the train. We would have had a night to sit next to each other in this dream station, and talk endlessly. Somehow I always wanted that. It was my dream."

"Guess what?"

"What?"

"Your dream just came true now."

"What!"

"Yes, we missed our train for today, like 15 minutes ago. I realized that, but I didn't care. I love the way it all came together to this moment, when we are talking about life. I simply couldn't get away from you."

"I am glad you didn't!"

"Who are we?"

"Where are we?"

"Is this love?"

"What do you think?"

"I think we will remember this night for a long time. We will reminisce it on a special night, again."

"That will be lovely!"

"This is lovely, too"

"You are lovely, actually."

"We are."

"You!"

"You."

It was more beautiful that we didn't end up speaking all night. In about 20 minutes, you said you felt sleepy. You leaned on my shoulder and slept like a baby. The next train to Chennai was 3 hours later. This time around, we were both travelling to Chennai, and we had an open ticket each. I remember all these only in hindsight now.

Back then, it was only that warm feeling of your left eye resting on my right shoulder. Of everything we had been speaking, the best part was the silence we shared. I was watching all those trains, the dream machines that kept stalling and moving in front of me. Your breath on my arms felt light. I felt heavy.

It was surreal. It was long. And it was at that moment when I felt so certain in my life that all I wanted was the night to not end, and the train not to arrive at all.

Never have I been so certain about anything else in my life.

Chapter 3.5

Being Human

"Do you see a pattern?" asked the blue star.

"I kind of do," said the pink star.

"From where they started, and the way they are it taking forward, there is a pattern but I don't know how to explain it..."

"I feel it is not just the movement forward but most importantly the journey backward into the memories that matters the most. Or should we say that the memories are going forward? Either way it is the language of reminiscence, and it is beyond explanations."

"I totally agree. Usually, I would love to differ. But this time I must confide that I am with you."

"As much as there is a pattern, there is randomness, too."

"That's how memories are... random, reckless and restless. You just can't control them, can you? They come in when they need to, and stay as long as they want to. You can either submit or surrender."

"That doesn't sound like a choice!"

"Is this a resolution that they are heading towards?"

"I'd call it a revelation of the self..."

"It all starts from self-realization, right?"

"There are two things – self-realization and self-image realization. You have to be flowing like water – shapeless, yet taking the form of the medium, to realize yourself in the process. The problem is that, most humans are driven by the image they want to build, and architect their selves according to it. Of what use is it in the long run?"

"We are asking too many questions to ourselves."

"Exactly."

"And that's important too. It is not in the answers that the solution lays, but in the world of conversations that a question yields. We need to ask more."

"Are we the stars? Or the souls? I am a little lost, given the way we are talking."

"You never know. I guess we all go through metamorphosis, the kind that the silk moth gets in, to become a butterfly."

"Change is not just inevitable, but beautiful too. The way it makes space for the new to thrive is essential. Forget the amazement, the very essential understandings are the most luxurious!"

"I can relate to this, almost like a human soul... On how it feels to understand the grandness of simplicity. It is always in the little things that the grandest happiness of life thrives. How does a kiss feel? How does a hug feel? I'd like to know."

"If only we could be humans..."

"If only they would be stars..."

Chapter 4

Can Love Happen Twice

SHE: (What is love?)

"Can love happen twice?"

I love asking this question, even though I know the answer.

There is a satiety attached to this habit of asking questions for which you know the answer. There is some kind of satisfaction and reassurance attached to it. Such moments of satisfaction are gems.

The scent of a headache roll-on, bursting the bubbles out of a wrapper, the sight of a crane in action, the country side scenery, cheese and wine, watching dominos fall, and on goes the large list of little things that make me oddly sufficed inside. Satisfaction is a luxury. Be it work or love, we yearn for a sense of satisfaction to keep going.

I guess this has been different in your case. You loved the extremes, and you were in for an adventure. For you, it was either an adventure or nothing. There was no space for mediocrity. There was no time for second thoughts. I was not so, but that didn't matter. I fell in love with you not just for what I liked in you but for what I saw in you, too. It was really magical, at least to me. Who wouldn't want to feel real and magical at the same time?

I was tired of bloated dreams and bleeding lies. I only wanted to feel close to reality, but still feel lured by the magic. I wanted to have that confidence on a soul that'd hold me right so I can fall to gravity or fly without the worry of getting hurt. I keep the flying part aside, and ask myself – 'When was the last time I fell freely?'

As kids, we had the courage to fall free on to the bed, or the wells, or the grasslands. But as we grow up, more than anything else, the fear of falling down naturally sets in. It is not the heights that we are afraid of, but the pain we'd feel after falling down that hurts and daunts. I've had enough falls to rise from.

I wouldn't call it falling in love, but I did fall for people in my life who always left me in shards, eventually giving me pain that was hard to revive from. They hurt. It hurt. When you came into my life, I knew it was nearly impossible that you and I would join hands to live a life together. I wasn't looking for an answer in you. You were an untamed question, and I felt happy to be that question mark which mattered. I never wanted you to complete me, but only accept me into your world.

Unlike me, I am not sure of how you had fallen for people in your life. But what I do know is how you loved a soul sincerely for five good years, and it was the most painful separation when you both parted ways. I still remember how you used to call me over phone and cry for hours. I wouldn't understand a word of what you said through the muffled cries, but always listened to your cries. It meant something in its own way, for you to cry out aloud and for me to be there for you. That is all that mattered.

A lot has happened over the last 4 years. We found love in each other, married, made some sense of living, and kept discovering each other constantly. We have talked about a million things, and one of them has always been the way you felt her presence in the places that we cross by. For instance, not one day have you missed saying this when we cross Alwarpet:

"Sigh, so many memories here with her. You know we used to breakfast at the Okadey restaurant every morning. I used to come all the way here, sit and stare at the tissue papers until she entered with that flawless smile. We'd talk a little, but mostly eat in each other's presence, and I'd leave to work after letting her go into her world. I had always been late to work on those days, but it never mattered. It feels like yesterday, but everything has changed. Okadey is not here, her company is not here, and she is not, either. Too many changes, all in such a short while."

Never has my indignation risen when you talk about her. Even if it did, I'd not show an ounce of my feelings outside. But I feel like asking this. Neither am I seeking an answer here nor am I going to interpret anything from what you would say. I already know. But I want to read what you'd say when I ask this.

Tell me, 'Can love happen twice?'

✳ ✳ ✳

HE: (The love of a Father)

Even before I answer your question, I am drawn to the kind of little moments that you talked about. I have my share of them, too. Like the smell of petrol, the scent of a new book, the sound of rain kissing the earth, the eyes of an elephant, the face of cows, the warmth in the sunrise, the zen in dim yellow evening lights, the sight of a peeled off orange, and it goes on.

I simply don't like to stop talking about this list, not only because it is nostalgic and but also because it is contemporary and brings out the child inside. The child inside, oh, I can't emphasize enough about its importance. If only we stopped pretending to be adults and live our lives like the kids that we are, life would be a lot simpler, and more beautiful. I must say I had the best childhood that I can imagine.

We lived in Hasthampatty, Kalaivanar Nagar, in a small cut road that was full of houses on both sides. As a blessing, the street teemed with kids of all ages. Fun was unlimited, and we grew up as a tribe that knew the freedom of being on the road. The sun, the sweat, the rain, or the cold… nothing stopped us from playing our hearts out. We were always out there, playing games with made-up rules that suited us. The fall of the evening was the only thing that made us enter homes.

Inside the house, it was appa and amma who made life even happier. I mean, there were no questions asked, especially from appa. amma to some extent was inquisitive, but appa was totally fine with whatever I did. The only time he took up a question seriously and asked me was when I told him that I am in love with you. In a very calm yet perturbed tone he asked me, "Can love happen twice?"

He had every right to ask that because, the first time I told him I was in love with her, he had not objected but tried to understand me more on how much I loved her and why I stood with my instincts. He knows the kind of pain I went through when we parted ways mutually, for all the questions that remained unanswered, and the uncertainty that prevailed.

Yes, her parents were caste-obsessed, not because they wanted to be, but because they were forced to be. Family was everything to them, and I don't complain. But then, it was not just their caste related world that kept her away from me. We had our differences of opinion and outlook in many critical things. She wanted an organized life with a good amount of certainty whereas I was dying to live an adventure that flirted with risks and creativity.

It was all good when we were two individuals loving each other from afar. But the very idea of beginning a life together created a rift between us. I don't blame her. She was the same ever since we knew each other. It was my eccentricity that was too hard to handle for her. Being in love and living together are two different things.

The ability to strike, share, and continue a conversation with a fellow soul takes a lot of heart. We are not used to that amount of unedited reality. We are only fascinated by the idea of living together. I wouldn't call it a breakup, what happened between us, but a new beginning for each of us to look beyond ourselves and the trance of love.

I still remember the last phone call conversation we ever had. After 120 minutes of seamless conversation, those final minutes of silence mattered a lot and then, I asked her.

"Can you live a happy life even if I am not in it?"

She didn't reply, but broke out into tears and cried for the rest of the conversation that seemed longer than it was. She told me how much she wanted to be with me, if not for all the pain that our love had caused her family. The kind of uncertainty where she had to throw everything behind and come over to me as family, and most importantly the fear of living with a peculiar person like me affected her decision.

You simply cannot make someone stay in love. In fact, you cannot make anyone happy at all. You can make someone smile or laugh temporarily, but their happiness is simply not in your control. It's their choice to make. You have no control over it. Happiness is a state of mind, and completely personal. I respected her feelings and accepted the reality.

We did talk this out. We parted like the rain and the rainbow. While we were together, we were so much meant for each other, and made life more beautiful than ever. But then, reality tore us apart. We tried to understand why departures are not always tied to sorrow. In the pain of separation lies the greater purpose of love, which is to set each other free.

Freedom is love. It wasn't easy for me. I know this. You know this. My parents know this. So naturally, when I said that I was in love with someone again, they froze.

My father had never been angry with me except for that one time when I was a child. And the memory stays etched in my mind. I was 4.5 years old then, and it was an early evening on a weekday, I think. appa had come home earlier, unusually. My friend Ahmed Ullah Khan and I were playing with a remote car. The battery seemed dull, and the car was staggering even when accelerated by the remote.

I took a look at appa, who sat on the cane chair in the hall, near the pale green coloured wall. We were living in a small rented house, but it was big enough for me to play my imagination. I was always building fictional characters, creating plots in my mind, and running around giving life to toys as courageous characters. So it was an action sequence that was in progress, and in a while the car stopped. The battery was dead.

I looked at appa again. He was sitting pinned to the chair with his elbows on his knees and hands on his head. I didn't know then, that it was a state of disturbed mind when someone sits like that with closed eyes and cupped hands on the face. I stood up, walked towards him, and reached out to his collar to ask, "Appa, battery". He sat still but I kept pulling at him.

As a kid, you know how relentless we always are. I kept repeating the same, "Appa, battery", over and over. In less than 30 seconds, I had asked for it 15 times, and he flipped. Yes, my appa who had never scolded me. For the first time ever, he lost his temper, took me over his shoulder, and went into the bedroom.

He threw me on the bed, and at first, I thought we were playing as he took a pillow and started hitting me like he usually did playfully. But a kid knows the truth, always, and it wasn't just play but a venting of anger that came along, and it hurt a bit. Not that it was particularly painful, but it was different because I had never felt anger from appa until then.

Ahmed was in the corner of the bedroom watching it all with a laugh, but the moment he realized appa was actually angry, he just ran way. I saw it through blurred eyes as I was bouncing around the bed when appa was throwing the pillow furiously at me, shouting, "Battery, battery?"

I cried due to the pain that the pillow caused, which marked the scene's end. appa had already rushed to hold me to his chest, lifted me and walked out to show outside sky that was lit the colour of blood. He was remorseful, and tried to make up for it with a kiss and a chocolate from Annachi's shop opposite our house. I did eat the chocolate, but somehow, a sense of fearful respect climbed upon me with regards to appa.

Everything changed from then. It wasn't days or months, but many years. I am yet to regain the friendly appa I had. That's not his fault, for it was only at that instance that he showed a tint of anger. He quickly came back to the person that he is - loving, caring and vulnerable with me. But it created a dent in me that refused to be corrected with time's healing magic.

I grew more respectful of him ever since then, but a different kind of love existed between us. We wouldn't talk much, but always understood each other. He still used to get me the best toys, and I continued to break them... He'd buy me new toys; I'd break them soon. He'd buy me more, and I'd break more. Nothing changed, but deep inside, my cell broke into pieces that never recouped.

Somehow, I have no regrets about that, for I changed as I grew up. And I kept a lot of secrets from appa. I was into the guilty pleasures of life, like sneaking 10 rupees from the cupboard for an ice cream, bunking a class to go out with friends, and all those little things piled up and made me maintain a distance from him all the time.

He was too perfect – that I couldn't face him with even a minute flaw. That's how it went. But never had he shown resentment towards anything. But unusually, when I told him that I was in love with you, after all the fiasco that we had gone through as a family after my first relationship, he was furious. We were in a bedroom again, but this time in the house that he had built out of his hard work.

A lot had changed but the kid inside me still remained as I stood there in a pensive mood facing my furious appa. He had just woken up. I roused him to talk about this. He was puzzled, lost in hope and chaos, as he uttered those words that you just uttered a while ago, too.

"Can love happen twice?"

There is nothing wrong in what he asked, for he wasn't someone who opposed love. He waved a green flag without question when I expressed my love for her years ago. He strived to make it work to the best of his ability. It was perfectly normal when he asked that, and I did try to explain why I wanted to live with you.

Everything that I said fell in as harsh contemporary words that he'd accept in a book, but not from his son. It was personal, and humiliating. More than anything else, he was exposed to the thought of 'what would the world think?'

I was never silent about my first relationship. I had mentioned it to my entire family, who believed it to be my destiny. They celebrated her and me as soul mates for this lifetime. They just accepted it as I had meant it. We are not talking about an overnight happening, but something that took time so naturally that it was rooted deep into their soul's soils that we would marry and live happily ever after.

'They are an ideal couple. How can they not be married?' was the thought of all my friends and family. For anyone to think of me falling in love for the second time would mean an irrational amount of hatred due to the cultural standards preached to us subconsciously. What is the use of culture if it doesn't celebrate the spirit of life, but confines us to notions of dress codes, diet and diligence? I was still the kid who feared pain and respected love. But this time, on the other side of the bed, I stood upright and exclaimed those words that are not mine but ours.

"Of course, it is not easy for you to comprehend what I am trying to explain. May be if I didn't remember that time when I was hurt inside by the blow of a pillow, I would have been more open, and we'd have been friends who shared everything openly. Somehow it didn't happen, and I don't blame you. Like I said, guilt, however small it is, was big enough to make me roll into my shell rather than being open outright. I was full of lies, not because I wanted to lie to you, but because I wanted to buy that inch of freedom that I needed.

"All I wanted to be was a free spirit that could love life as a miracle, and leave no stone unturned, to experience every extreme adventure. It was a feeling that I wasn't in control of, the rush of instincts that guided me through the course of life. I felt like water that flows, taking the shape of the path. It was all that I needed, to be with the flow. What has it got to do with the calm and composed nature of amma and you? I did not wish this to come to this level and hurt you, nor did I expect an easy yes to what I proposed".

Somehow I stalled, feeling stranded in the middle of the two souls who had raised me with all the love and care. Yes, amma was standing by his side all the time. An hour earlier, I had said the same to her and made her realize how much I was in love with the soul that I claimed was too precious to be explained. She looked convinced and had led me to talk to appa.

But in his presence, she had her stand aligned to appa. Why won't she? We tend to stand by our loved ones, don't we? How was I to explain the inexplicable? How was I to justify that it wasn't pleasure that I was seeking but purpose? How could I make him understand that it is not about love but something much beyond that? I was full of words yet short of a chance. With the same intensity of that pillow that crushed me onto the bed years ago, I took the pain of helplessness to my heart and broke into tears like I did back then.

I went into the restroom and cried out loud, looking into the mirror with nothing but the raging anger about my inability to explain magic to appa. How can magic be explained? It can only be felt. Maybe it takes time for him to understand, or maybe it was just a matter of time before everything fell in place. But I wasn't going to let time decide again. With a washed face and tears that refused to stop, I came out to the bedroom, looked at him, and said,

'Appa, I know it is hard for you to hear this. I know I don't sound right to you, and I had never sounded so. We've been through this already. With all due respect, there is no one more important than you and amma in my life. Let us not forget that it was you who raised me as this soul that wanders, questions, ponders, and explores. Why do I feel like holding you accountable for the state that you are in now? I mean, I am your son, and here I am, standing for what I want.

In fact, I don't want this. I need this. I need her. The relationship we share might sound irrational to you now, but eventually you will understand the purity and permanence of this. I want you to trust me this time, appa, more than ever. I am sure of this, and I can reassure you of the happiness I'd get if I live with her for this lifetime. And to answer your question, forget about once or twice. In my eyes, love just happens and keeps happening. I don't think it can be contained; let alone be a commitment to one soul.

What is love after all? An attraction, desire, physics, chemistry, calling, destiny, or marriage? There simply is so much to relate to, but nothing seems definite, does it? It is shapeless, limitless, and infinite. Like when we stood together in the waves of the sea, they approach and retreat constantly. We looked forward to the wave that'd hit our toes in a second, and look back at the wave that retreats, taking a part of us to the vast ocean. How warm is this?

I am not talking only about the warmth of holding hands together, but more importantly about the warmth of the Sun that keeps rising. It keeps burning itself into the space, to win the souls that witness it. That's love, like the one found in the smiling child, the crying clouds, the musical butterfly, the silent ant, the sensational soil, the sensible books, the stirring movies, and the satin memories...

I love it when I get into this flow of things, or should I say, when things flow into me, and I no longer feel myself but the thoughts that I intend to express. Love is not just in the air, but everywhere. I see her in all of these, and I see all of these in her. What can I do, appa?'

He took a deep breath, searched for water, then took another minute to comprehend it, and came up with that million-dollar question,

"Okay, I can hear that you are very much in love with this girl, but I don't trust this yet. I don't trust you. I don't know what your definition of love is. I leave it to you. You always wanted to be a writer, may be you can write about it in your books. To me, you are that little child still, whom I raised. I don't know, it is a different kind of pain inside, now. You'll understand when you have your child, how it is to be put in such a situation.

"I prefer to stay neutral now, and not ask or tell you anything anymore, for I can see you are not in a state to listen. You have a lot to tell, and I can hear it all. But I am afraid that is not going to change anything. I have nothing more to say, but one question does arise... now you come over and tell me that you are experiencing love with a soul and that you want to live together. What is the certainty that you won't feel the same thing with another soul down the line? How can I believe that you won't come and stand in front of me saying that you are in love again?"

I replied instantly,

"Yes, appa. You are right about this. I might meet some special soul and fall in love all over again. I might very well experience the wave of magic in more than one soul hereafter. I am not denying it. That would be lying to myself, which I can't afford to do. But having said all that, I will never come and stand in front of you asking your consent to marry that soul into my life. I realize that love and marriage are two different things. Both are beautiful, and interdependent.

Fortunately, for now, I feel both in one soul. I don't know if I will feel this way with any other soul. Life is art, and you will see for yourself on how I love life inside out. For now, I don't expect you to answer me affirmatively. I am happy that you've heard me out with uninterrupted attention. You let me speak, and you listened. You even fought with me. This, to me, is an intense form of love! I shall wait."

He didn't say a word, but stood up and walked into the restroom. Why did it feel like me walking past myself? That's it. Pretty much for a month after that, we didn't speak at all! As loud as the silence was, it somehow felt comfortable, too.

And after a couple of months, appa and amma had decided to go to your house to talk about our marriage. May be it is a matter of time that we have to see what happens when it happens. They didn't go with a question, but with an answer that we were meant for each other. When I came to know about this sweet, grand gesture of his to break through his barriers and reach out to make my dream come true, that heavy memory of the pillow fight from decades ago seemed to feel light.

Somehow, I felt like I earned the appa I had before that incident. He gifted me the opportunity to fall in love with him in a different way, again. That moment when he put me before his egos, only to make sure I was happy and content – it felt like all the shards had come together to create a mirror that held the reflection of that particular moment.

✳ ✳ ✳

SHE: (Breaking down happily)

How powerful is a memory recited, even though it is repeated? I asked you because I wanted to hear from you. Somehow it feels liberating to just listen to you. And the tail does carry the sting, doesn't it? Of everything you said, I am stuck in that moment when your parents had come home to visit us. My parents were informed beforehand, and we were cleaning the house that morning. You know that mood where you clean up the entire house in full speed, and you get to see how beautiful your home is with a little order?

Before I could finish feeling satisfied, your parents entered. In your eyes, there was a different kind of joy attached to this, for all your questions were answered. To me it was a different kind of pleasure that rooted from the pain of having kept it all to myself ever since I knew you. I am referring to talking to you, seeing you, or kissing you for the first time. This was about the first time I got to know you. I don't know when it happened, but I do remember the way I felt loved and confident and carefree at that moment.

I was in love, but I just wouldn't admit that because you were in a relationship already. It was difficult to love a soul so much in silence and that pierced me ruthlessly over time. I bore it all. Even after we expressed the intent to live together, I felt the silence, for there were obstacles still to cross. And they were not external, but our own loving families that had their share of time to come to terms. And not to forget the way we got to know each other in a scary pace amidst all this.

It was the first time for me, to think of living with someone forever, and I was in sync with it positively. That scared me. But you had an experience already and I was wondering, out of love and care, how the marriage thing was hitting you. I wasn't sure of how this worked altogether; it still feels hazy. That moment when your appa and amma came in, your amma dragged a chair close to me, sat by my side and held my hands...

I broke into tears, and couldn't speak a word. But I conveyed a whole lot than words could. A quick flash of memory came in, when you held my hands on the streets as we walked after you proposed that we live together. I felt close to you, even though you were not there. And I wanted to come running into you. We were almost there, close to the possibility of sleeping and waking up in each other's arms every morning.

Sun and the moon, you and me...and you feel us both as I imagine this moment filled with warmth and chillness? Love, it is. Love, is!

Chapter 5

Love In (And) Lust

HE: (The feeling called Lust, and the first kiss)

That's really touching. All of a sudden, I feel your touch. I am drawn to how magical it is to feel each other's body for the love of it. There is love in lust, and lust in love. Our bodies are magical mediums that reflect the space of the universe. Our eyes hold the moon and the black hole. Our arms are hills that bend to the beds of our bellies and flow into the movement of our wiggling toes. There, the inch of what we feel is lovely.

There is geography in the curves, physics in the resonating vibes, chemistry in the rising hormones, and character in the face art. There is so much of art and science in our body. To realize it means to surrender to it completely. What more than giving it all only to feel full, and taking it all to feel empty? Sex, intercourse, merging souls, making love… Either way, they all convey the same meaning.

The difference lies in the way the society wants to view it. Pre-marital, post-marital, safe, unsafe, and so many more hashtags that come attached when two souls collide with each other. I am turned on as I write this. What is the first reaction that an average human will have to this statement? It is perfectly natural to experience a surge of emotions and hormones at the cost of those vibes.

The social conditioning has made us so reluctant to experience love physically before marriage. It is considered sane to talk about love, but when we speak about making love, well… Our hormones flourish in the ages between 18 and 24, precisely when we are asked to stay intact, and refuse anything beyond words!

What if we had the freedom to experience each other with societal consent? Will that change the way we view lust or harness the way we feel love? Will it reduce the crimes that happen in the name of forbidden temptations? Will it make life more beautiful? We have started talking about it, and it is no longer taboo. But honestly, we are not ready to accept the curiosity it stirs in the minds of the young people.

How can the most beautiful and the basic instinct not be discussed at all, let alone experienced? It is very tricky to centralize or structure a stream of education to teach this. It is simply impossible to achieve the goal of enlightening minds.

Educated? Yes, they will be. Enlightened? Hard to say.

How will you ever put into words what can only be felt? One has to feel his/her body, embrace the world of vibes that they come with, control the energy that it unleashes, learn, and unlearn. A sexually active soul understands love more than a dormant one that speaks about social values and statues inside the temples.

Just my opinion that there is a lot of divinity in the way life builds up to the moment of orgasm, and everything goes blank in the rise and the fall. Even if it is for a few seconds, everything around goes black, and it is just that wave of inexplicable pleasure that sails through the body, connecting you to the stars in the universe that twinkle brighter.

Every twinkle is an orgasm reflected. One huge stardom of emotions up in the air all the time. That is why I love the night – it takes the lighter skin off the sky, and shows us the naked universe full of magic. How to name this?

On the context of lust, I feel fortunate to have experienced the world of love intensely with you. It was our habit to experience and appreciate each other in every possible way. The way you hold me by my face when we look into each other's eyes, the way I hold you closer when you slip away from my approaching kiss, how you kept your eyes open when I came closer to kiss you, and how I kept staring into your eyes, beating the urge to kiss you… my heart beats faster now.

Nothing really dies in the world of love, let alone memories. It is like an open space that keeps blossoming, with dreams and destinies tied to the garland of time and space. I would not see lust as anything beyond what it is. In the songs I loved, and the people I was infatuated with, there always was this tint of lust hidden like a seed.

And then, you happened. Everything changed.

I got to know how assuring a hug is, how reassuring a kiss would be. Things about myself that I'd never have known until I had a soul to share it with. Sex is empowering in the way it liberates and belies the notions of the society pressed deep in our minds. It doesn't educate, it enlightens.

It breaks you totally, and makes you, too. Every part of making love is a universe within a universe.

I am reminded of the first time we kissed. And our conversation about the same after years, when we cuddled after midnight, past a fully burnt candle.

"I love kissing you."

"I love kissing you, too."

"Are they both same?"

"The way you kiss me and how I kiss you?"

"No, I am not talking about you and me. I am asking about kissing and being kissed. Are they two different things? I mean, when we kiss, it is both our lips that do the talking. But why is there a difference of feeling while we take turns?"

"It is in giving and taking. I guess there is a difference in the way I love you, and you love me. There is a difference in how you cup me and how I do that. Everything is different. Nothing in this world is same at all, especially when it comes to two souls in love."

"It's such a lie when people say that two souls are so much one as each other. I place more faith in the contradictions rather than the similarities."

"But there are moments when we feel as one when we kiss each other, don't we?"

"Of course, after that initial time of taking turns, and touching with soft thrusts, there is a time when it melts down to the dwindling space."

"Many times it feels like the first time to me, when we kiss each other."

"There is a birth in every kiss. There is death of time and space every time the lovers' lips meet."

"True."

"Need not be."

"Then?"

"I'd say it's magical."

"I believe in magic."

"You are magical."

"You are my magic."

We ended up kissing each other, again, before either of us could reply. I am now lost in the track of time, and all I could see is your lips that await the touch of my love, and the breath that warms up. Our very first kiss many years ago feels like a lifetime apart, yet close.

The walls, the windows, and everything around faded, and the only thing that made its way into me was the running train's sound in the track nearby. I vividly remember the way I came closer, breaking your anticipation, holding you closer, cupping your face, and feeling your presence. Your first touch on me was magical, and it felt like a trance that I wasn't able to come over or didn't want to come over.

Instead, I chose to come close enough that our noses touched and far enough that our lips missed each other. In this finite space thrives the language of the lips, holding the unspoken words and the untold love. Not that it shouldn't be, but that it can't be. It felt so surreal when our breaths met and our lips brushed occasionally.

God, what is there in the way our breaths play? It is so intense and we were yet to know it. There was a deep, mesmerizing feeling, when I breathed in your breath. And when I touched your soft lips and felt you, everything cut loose. All I could think of was the next moment where I would hold you close and kiss you.

Yes, our lips met. We met. Our lips loved. We lived. There was a gentle feeling in the way I kissed you. It is the reflection of the yearning that I always want with you. It is a very different kind of feeling that I am not able to come past. It is like I could taste your entire self in the kiss. The friction of the touch, the fraction of the second, and the fiction of the yearning – there simply is so much to dream about.

Life is beautiful. You are beautiful. I have so much more to say about this. I wish I could. How to name this?

✳ ✳ ✳

SHE: (Love can't be possessed)

Every word you said kissed me sincerely, touched me gently, and moved me fiercely. How powerful is a word? Its ability to be read and felt on the whole, its power to persuade and hold you in its wake. Every word is a world, and to belong to it, is to be. Words carry both the sound of solitude and the music of companionship. More of this is felt when we kiss each other.

In the first few prints of the lips on each other, it is the self-love that rises. The souls are excited to express how much they love each other. In a while, the individuality crumbles, and it's no longer about two souls expressing each other, but one intense song of the universe that they are singing together. Every kiss is a song, full of words that the universe sneaks through the notes of the breath that stays lit throughout.

How to name this? I don't think you can name this feeling.

We are obsessed about names. Brand names, social media handle names, product names, pet names… Do you realize that the largest lies we ever keep telling to ourselves are our names? Take a second to think of why you are called what you are. It is because your parents named you so, and everybody then called you so. Slowly you got used to the idea and responding to anyone who called you so.

Does this name belong to you? Or define you? Who are you? Do we need a name to define each other? Souls don't have names or an identity. We don't call each other by names. We only know each other. We are connected by feelings, and the feeling called love that is manifested into all the other feelings like happiness, hatred, dreams, success, failure, goals, games, passion, etc.

I guess we all should have two names: one kept since birth, and the other we keep for ourselves when we realize who we are inside. It is not a race, but a pursuit; the journey to discover the purpose. There is so much pressure in this journey, is there not? It is not just the adventure out in the open world, but the walks and runs through the closed streets of commerce and the corporate world that takes up our time.

I don't feel any of this when I kiss you. The onus to feel important or to earn a name for myself stands torn only to reveal the skin inside me. A naked soul is the most sophisticated fabric that there is.

Happiness is reading through these words, and living the life that flourishes in the space between them. I look forward to a lot of that. The pursuit is always towards happiness, right? We are so used to being happy and yearn to be happier, that anything other than feeling good hurts. But the problem is that the spectrum of feelings is so wide. There is more to life than happiness. There are so many emotions. Everything is to be lived. And everything is so intense.

Like an embarrassment that tears you apart from your carefully constructed image. How intense is that? Would you love to experience that and evolve as a better soul or try to shy away saying 'life is all about the pursuit of happiness'?

Happiness settles. And settlement is no progress in the long run. Has anything great ever been achieved through a happy mind? Of course, peace is attained as the immediate by product. But that again is a feel good factor. Real peace is much more than that, and involves layers of chaos to arrive at, truly. For this precise reason, I am not a big fan of happiness. To me it is a slow poison that makes you stall and contemplate rather than move and discover.

Souls in love understand this. I understand this.

Our relationship has been full of such diverse emotions, extreme and eccentric. Never has there been a dull day. A terrible day is better than a normal day is what you believe in. It took a long time for me to understand the outlook you have toward emotions. You are a very emotional person. You know how to make me cry, but at the same time you'd also know how to receive a tear. It was painful for me earlier to confront all this.

Confrontation is one thing that I found so difficult. I knew who you are, and what you come with. You never cared to keep me happy but mostly ecstatic. You never tried to give me calm, and instead broke the hell out of the chaos to gift me enlightenment. You were my teacher. That's how I used to feel you inside.

The tough way in which you taught me how beautiful and cruel emotions can be. At many instances it hurt painfully. But in the pain came a realization that was more important than happiness. Pain gives birth to sense and sensations. To confront you in these moments when you hurt me was the most important thing that happened to me in this life. I know no one else can or will love you as much as I do, and I love none but you with all my heart.

I agree that love is no one's possession but the universe's own. It flows through an open mind, and empowers you to live more beautifully than ever. But I couldn't accept you loving any other soul at any degree ever. I wasn't so before marriage, but what changed me? I don't know. It just felt strange to share you with any other soul, however small the instance.

But deep inside I always knew that I could never contain you, and even if I did, it wouldn't suffice. I wanted you to be free, but I couldn't let you be. Aargh, I hate myself for being this ping-pong ball of pensive motion. The pace at which I fall to and fro unto you is scary. As much as I confront you, I realize it is not just you who I am confronting, but myself. My thoughts about you reflect how I think rather than what I think.

This realization is vital. I am in this constant confrontation with myself every time I confront you. Why is it so hard to do that to one's self? Is it because it is tough? Or is it because it hurts? I guess it is the pain that we are afraid of, not the act. We are not afraid of heights but of falling down. I am getting to realize that slowly.

I am beginning to understand that every emotion is equally important.

* * *

HE: (Two Important instances)

We don't feel any of this pain after we are dead, do we? Death enthrals me. Thinking about death makes me gather the sense of living into the basket of time. What happens after we are dead? Our bodies come to rest, our eyes are static, and everything stalls. But what about our conscience? A very common curiosity, and the unknown is always inquisitive. If at all there is God, where is He/She?

Speaking of God, I am reminded of two intense instances now. 3 years ago, I was directing a film about the world of Autistic adults who came together to start a bakery on their own. SAI BAKERY was the name, and it was a transforming experience to be with them and shoot their journey. The moments we spent with them were so important. So there was this instance when it was raining, and I took a break to come out and nature's bounty touch the ground.

Only in nature does a fall feel so quintessential. Be it rain or sunset, the fall is beautiful. So on that day, as I was standing lost in the falling rain which kissed everything it touched, Srinivasan joined me. The 18-year-old soul was diagnosed with ADHD and a world of complications, but that was on the outside. His soul was the most curious and the healthiest I had ever seen, and there we were, standing together and watching the rainfall. It was an appeasing experience.

"What are you looking at?" he asked looking ahead.

"I am looking at the rain falling down so beautifully," I said, looking ahead too.

He usually asks a lot of questions. It is not that he doesn't know the answers. He asks to reassure himself.

"Why do you think it rains?" he asked me curiously.

"I don't know, you tell me," I replied, even more curiously.

"It is because we don't water the plants properly. And God opens the tap from above to water them all!"

"Really?"

"Really!"

"Where is God?"

"Inside,"

"Inside?"

"Yes, inside!"

"Inside where?"

"Inside the house, right there in my cupboard!"

"What do you say? I have been searching for him everywhere. Show me where he is..."

"I meet him every morning and night. He is my best friend but just that he wouldn't talk. He is dumb. Come on in, I'll show you."

He held my hands, led me to his cupboard, and showed a statue of Sai Baba. He said that he talked to Him every day and night, in vain, for that God never spoke back. Right then he was talking to his God about how his day was, how it was raining outside, and how the plants were so happy. And in the end, he touched my forehead to bless me with the goodness. I had to hold back my tears with a lot of effort.

I was speechless in the seconds that followed. I stood there, helpless, and questioned. A soul with all the answers had left me with questions.

The second instance was more powerful. I was directing another video, and this time it was for the Chennai Children's Choir. We were shooting interviews of a bunch of kids who came from marginalized backgrounds, and stood united in their love for singing. There was this interview where a 1st grade kid was to be shot next. The lights were being set up. I had this habit of talking to them in between shooting scenes.

 "Just a few more minutes. We'll get started. Let's play a game while we wait," I said with a smile.

"I love games, yes tell me," she said with a bigger smile. Her eyes were bright and lit the studio space more than the actual lights did.

"Let's imagine that you go to sleep tonight and when you wake up in the morning, God is sitting beside you. He is asking for one wish that will be granted to you for this lifetime. What will you ask for?"

"I will ask him a question."

"What is that?"

"I will ask him why he is not at all coming to Earth these days!"

 "What do you mean he is not coming to Earth only these days?"

"Yes, have you not heard of Mahabarata? There are so many gods who fought evil. Today there is so much evil out there, but where are the gods hiding?"

"Who told they were hiding?"

"My science teacher. I asked her, where the gods are, and why we can't see them at all now. She told that they were playing hide and seek, and will come out at the right time. I keep searching for the gods every time we play hide and seek. They are not at all there. I mean there is a limit to hide, right?"

I was perplexed on hearing these words from a 5 year-old. Is there anything wrong in what a child asks with an open heart? Just because we are not able to answer doesn't make the question invalid.

These two instances with the kids shoved a different kind of love into myself.

Would life be so complex were it not for all the lies that we've invented and sold? Lies triumph too. Decorated with dignity and desire, we are consuming and contemplating lies every second. Maybe life is all about discovery. And the moment we started inventing, the complications came along.

The invention of the wheel is the single most important discovery that led to transportation, exploration, colonization, to super powers, wars, greed, technology, inequality, insecurity, and what not? No one knew the power that wheel had to revolutionize the entire lifecycle. All these stories, dreams, and memories; they all yearn to end in a photograph ultimately.

The obsession to post rather than live, the passion to lure than attract, the need to be popular more than content, are taking all of us for a ride. We are all in it, for the pat on the back, and the grip of the golden watch. Adrenaline chasing junkies and acknowledgement seeking monkeys. Soon, we don't know what the hell we are doing with our life.

Take a look around for a second; the kind of routine we are in, the jobs we do, the things we sacrifice, the sleep we lose, and the sunrises we miss. Social media connects us all, but also detaches us from ourselves ruthlessly. Let's admit the itch to scroll and like and comment, or worse, share.

If only we could stop this maze of digital world, our vision will come out of the vertical or horizontal modes. My fingers ache, and my lips are dry. I wish you could hold me in your lips, and water me with your fingers. That is all the salvation the world needs too. Love, more of love that stirs.

Right now, I need you.

* * *

SHE: (Sex and the Self)

Remember the conversation we had about sex and the self?

"What is self?" I asked, polishing my nails sitting in the balcony.

"To understand the self, you have to understand ego," you said watching me intently.

"Go on, enlighten me,"

"That freedom of the joy you have when you dance naked in the bathroom is self. And that immediate thought stalling your dance when you realize that there's someone watching through the keyhole, is ego."

"Embarrassing?"

"Embracing!"

"But that is totally wrong, I feel. Ego need not always be seen in a negative connotation. Ego is what builds up, and makes us. We learn from what we see, hear, and go through. In that sense, isn't ego an important element of our survival?"

"That's the problem. Often we survive, forgetting the fact that we are born to thrive. I am not talking about the urge to rise beyond and fly high. I mean, it is the most basic thing to be a free spirit. And we have too many layers in the name of learning. We forget what we are inside, and the answer often lies inside. Everyone here is ashamed of who they are, but not of the fact that they are not who they claim to be."

"But eventually we all strike a sweet spot between the self and ego. It's when we realize our self and move on stronger, to become what we are meant to be. Sometimes making a living is an art by itself, with all the chaos and character meeting each other and smiling gleefully."

"Are we realizing our self, or our self-image? Often, we are stuck with an image of ourselves that we want to believe in. We are a generation raised by television and social media, made to believe in the power of an image rather than the vulnerability of self, the colour of a fabric rather than the texture of the skin, the speed of the vehicles rather than the silence of the lambs, the call of duty rather than the music of the sparrows. One whole lifetime is meant to build an image, try to save it, and be it."

"Can love break these shackles?"

"Can sex break these walls?"

"Why do you think there are walls?"

"The same reason you think about the shackles. I guess it comes in different forms, the discrimination that we offer to ourselves."

"Is sex an ultimate answer to all the questions?"

"I don't know. May be that's why it is so powerful because it doesn't seek an answer, but still explores to explode into an unknown space of liberation."

"What is sex?"

"You tell me."

"We both will."

"Sex is a duet of the self and ego!"

"Sex is what binds the self and ego."

"Sex is when the ego starts flirting and sheds its skin, slow and whole, to surrender to the naked self that experiences it all."

"Sex is where the self, starts kissing the ego, and embraces the layers of existentialism with no questions asked."

"There are questions, though, in the journey."

"But there are no complaints, at least when two souls make love to each other, truly."

"Sex is a game,"

"Sex is a game."

"Who wins?"

"It is not about winning, but the fight that matters!"

"You mean love?"

"And making love?"

"Aren't they different?"

"Aren't they the same?"

"There is a fight in both."

"But doesn't fight mean pain?"

"That's the best part of it,"

"This is intense, just to talk and be heard. Do you hear the breeze that keeps hearing us out too?"

The breeze came in, louder and softer, bringing us back to the magic. What if magic is the natural state and we are all stuck in the rut of reality unnaturally? What if the mad souls make the true sense of life and sanity is a disease? I looked into you, and you knew that even before you looked onto me. The weight of my vision was landing upon your cheeks like a butterfly whose last wish was to flutter by the side of your breath.

We kept looking at each other, and we kind of lost track of time. There was confrontation in the way you looked at me, and appeasement in the way I slid into it. There was a fight in the way we kept looking into each other, and surrender when we blinked. The breeze carried us far away into the closest of our self. In the subtlest moments as these at ease, our souls understand what it feels to stay connected without a wireless network.

There was a loud thunder that faded into the skies. Like a flower that blossomed, we both smiled slowly as we kept looking into each other. It felt so intense that I wanted to run into you, but I didn't. The little distance between us burnt so hard, and felt so far.

God, I was turned on!

Is this love? Before we could answer this, there came a faraway raindrop, falling onto us by destiny.

"Nature just had its orgasm," I said.

"And so did our eyes," you said.

You laughed out loud. We reached out to each other. Our hands knew how to hold on to the moment. We spent the rest of the evening cuddling, and watched the rains fall onto the buildings that the humans have built all around. Somehow, we were seeing all the trees between them.

We were reading between the lines.

We were hearing the music of the rain's kiss.

We were in love.

Chapter 5.5

The Flow In Our Stars

"Oh, I could feel the moisture of that rain amidst all the fire in me," said the pink star.

"I am amazed and surprised at the way they had loved conversations," exclaimed the blue star.

"Go on, finish what you want to say. I know the pain in waiting to be heard!"

"You bet. I clearly see that these two souls have fallen in love over each other, head over heels, Mars onto Venus, magic over reality, all of this and more, purely through conversations. How can two souls who loved each other so much through conversations face a drought in the same, grow distant, and fall apart? However small or big it might be, a creek is a creek. I just don't understand."

"I am not sure. We have to step back and listen to them to understand,"

"I loved the way they spoke about self-realization and self-image actualization. At times, I feel so angry looking at their fairness cream advertisements that I want to burn the hell out of those tubes!"

"But there is enough global warming already…"

"Come on, don't get me started on that. If only these humans avoid plastic in their household and in their smiles, the Earth would be a lot cooler!"

"That is some truth melting down,"

"When was the last time we fought?"

"We are stars. Stars don't fight!"

"Why not? This is a problem. This is their problem, too. They live for such a short while yet they are always concerned about their images, and do everything they can to build an identity. They are obsessed with their identities. They believe themselves to be something, and they strive so hard to actuate that dream. The secret is, there are no identities or differentiation or uniqueness! Snowflakes melt. So does the human body. They are the same organic matter that keeps dying every minute. The question is, how are they going to make it count? They all have a purpose, and how I wish they remain calm instead of becoming characterized, to let the universe talk to them too, as much as they try so much to talk to the universe. There are meditation and the drugs and the books, all those attempts to connect with the universe, yet they don't understand the importance of stepping back and listening, like you told. It is often as simple as that, to stop controlling things and to observe the flow and be one with the flow. Everything else falls into place. It just does!"

"That is a powerful revelation, and I just shone a whole lot more. Humans who are star gazing now would have been thrilled…"

"I can see the twinkle in their eyes already. They just want to be overwhelmed all the time, don't they?"

"Oh my universe, I feel human now."

"There's nothing wrong in feeling human. They feel the same way too at times. Like they feel the stars inside them every now and then. We are all one and the same in this universe. You do realize that don't you?"

"Hard to differentiate!"

"Stop differentiating!"

"I don't feel like a star anymore…"

"What do you feel?"

"I feel the love!"

Chapter 6

Intensity Of Innocence

HE: (You are my Saraswati)

What is love? I truly don't know. But I feel close to it. These instincts have guided me towards you. I'm not trying to define love, but trying to listen to what this moment says to me. I now have this strong instinct to share a dream that I remember. I was always full of dreams, literally. I don't mean the ambitious way. I dream almost every day, and I remember it often after waking up. Few of them stay stamped in my memory, like forever.

I was studying in kindergarten then. It was the school's Sports Day, and I had won the first prize in the 'Pick and Place Potato'. A game where a steel ring with 6 potatoes inside it will be placed. About 20 meters apart, a similar ring will be set up but without potatoes, for each participant. On the whistle, the participants have to pick one potato, run and place it in the empty ring, come back, pick another one and repeat. I had a fast foot. I won.

Winning feels good. It sets you free. On winning, I was fast asleep after the long day, and this dream happened.

During midnight, a whirring breeze woke me, and the concrete ceiling opened up. The way you'd open your drawer, the ceiling opened up from top to bottom. The full moon shone like usual. It was mesmerizing to see such light and before I could blink, the clouds came down as a mass of specific shapes to touch my nose. I breathed a sigh and they moved slightly upwards. I sat up and looked to the sky.

The clouds had formed the shape of a series of steps, from my home's ceiling till the sky. I stood up, took the first step, then the second, and the third. I lost count after that as I reached the top. The steps suddenly ended, and I was in this misty space with a lot of white smoke around. I was reminded of my grandfather, Velusamy, then. The only time I had seen such a beautiful shape of smoke was when he smoked his cigar.

In the evenings, after I reached home after school, I would run into his room to talk about the day. He'd be standing serenely amidst the white clouds. I had to wade past them, and he'd know I was near and he'd throw the cigar away to lift me out of the clouds and into the living room. He is my inspiration in so many ways, and he helped me prepare the first ever speech I delivered later in the 3rd grade, during the school morning assembly. It was about punctuality.

His handwriting superimposes all these clouds, and lands into me as a painful memory that he is no more with me.

Getting back to the dream... I was facing the endless horizon of something white. Slowly, the clouds withered, and I saw a lady sitting on a lotus. At first glance, she was calling me towards her with open arms. I didn't know her, I hadn't seen her before that. Yet I walked closer. Her arms were still stretched wide. What is more beautiful than the warmth of open arms? I went close, almost at a touchable distance.

She was draped in a pink saree that looked a lot like the lovely lotus that she was sitting upon. Her face was bright in an overpowering way and before I knew it, she hugged me and kissed my cheeks. She then made me stand in front of her, and searched for something in one of the lotus petals. She took out a cup of talcum powder, and started dabbing my cheeks with a powder-puffed sponge.

I was in my neatly ironed school dress then, tucked in and ready to take on the world. After the unexpected make over, she wished me, "Go on, and win this day!"

Suddenly, the clouds disappeared, and I was on a free fall to my bed. I woke up gasping, like you would when you wake up from a sky diving dream. It was my first sky dive. I survived, searched for my breath, and fell asleep again. But I did remember the dream the next morning. I told it to all my friends, but no one believed me. I tried explaining it to my parents too, but they couldn't figure out who that lady was.

Almost a month went by, I guess. One day, I saw this image of the same lady on a lotus in a calendar that appa had brought home. I ran jumping up to him and shouted out to the lady in the picture. I explained the connection to my dream. amma was excited, in particular. It happened to be goddess Saraswati, supposedly the Hindu goddess of knowledge, music and art.

"How lucky you are my son! Goddess Saraswati herself has blessed you with a powder puff! She is an angel and will always look after you, forever."

"What about Jesus ma?"

Back then, I was studying in a Christian school. I still remember how they rolled out a poster of Kali and asked the 600 odd students to count the number of skulls She held in her hand. And they pointed out the blood splash on her face, equating her to Satan, who killed people. A week later, they showed a poster of Ganesha alongside that of an elephant. We were asked to find 5 similarities, which we did. Then we were told that he was not a God, but a mere animal. Thus my introduction to Hindu gods was a strange door that never opened.

So when amma was telling all the more about goddess Saraswati, I didn't buy it. I didn't know or trust Her. I moved on. But I didn't get past that dream. I held on to it. Years later, when I grew to be a rational soul that didn't submit to discrimination of any form, I wondered how absurd the teachers at my primary school had been. We were brainwashed.

I have nothing against Christianity or Jesus, though. In fact, if you ask me who my best friends are, the immediate names that would pop up are Lillian and Roselyn. It is impossible to put into words the kind of friendship I share with them and how much I miss them right now. It is just that the way certain people have made an effort to infuse religion into souls that startles me.

I was nearly an atheist later on, but I still loved this dream when goddess Saraswati powder puffed me. Somehow did not seem like a God, but a person who truly cared about me. Every time I felt down or depressed, this dream would rise in my mind's temple, and I'd be submitting to it. However heavy I was, this dream would set me free. It would make me fall in love with the kid inside me, the one that I managed to keep alive within me all the way through.

I was scared to talk about it to anyone, and I didn't believe in angels at all, until you happened. I have mentioned this and all the more crazy dreams to you. I didn't care how you responded. Sharing with you was enough for me. I didn't expect answers, just the listening ears. You'd understand me beyond what I tried to express. It is like wanting to learn more than what they teach you.

You were wisdom, and ignorance. You were light and also darkness. I saw everything in you. I started to feel you more than what I spoke with you or heard from you. I started inhabiting this universe that was you. In an open space of endless white, you felt like an insistent constant coffee stain that kept spreading all over.

I didn't know what you meant to me or how you entered my life, but I believed in the stain that your soul spread on mine. I looked upon you subconsciously and leaned onto your mind like a sunflower does to its sun. Blissful music sweeps into me and I break down in tears. You are my Saraswati.

* * *

SHE (Speak to me about Separation):

You talk so much about the dreams in general, and the one that came true in particular. To me, you are a dream that I never saw coming. I feel like I've told you this already, déjà vu, but what's the harm in stressing on something that feels so light? Of all the certainty that I had with you, holding your hands for this lifetime was the last thing I could wish for.

I did wish for it though, secretly. You heard it. We heard it. But neither of us did anything about it. Yet here we are, bound together to love and fight with a free spirit. My mind leaps to the way you hold my hand when driving the car, walking down the street, winking at the star lit sky, wanting to be held after a misunderstanding and it goes on.

Can you feel the warmth already? I love the touch, and the friction of this beautiful second that seems longer than it is. Is it because of the time that is less, or is it timeless? I don't care about the reason behind it. I care about you. You are my answer, and my question...

There are instances when I have felt this burning distance between us, raring to bring us together and burn us to ashes. Many times in this life, I have wished to die. I wouldn't do that, but I had wished. Is death one's destiny? Or a desire to be born again? Either way, that's how I feel when I am away from you. Sometimes all I need is your presence, if not by my side, at least around me.

I can live with that. It makes me feel alive, like you feel when you are standing on the Kandy Hills in Sri Lanka and looking at the sun setting on a serendipitous evening. Peace accumulates when I am with you physically. Yes, we are always connected as souls. But the warmth of the actual presence is something else. You always loved me intensely, but you were often gone when I needed you the most.

I knew I can never completely have you, even though we are married, I know I can never own you. I am not happy that way, but accepting of it, because you are happy that way. You are a free spirit. I adore you for that. But I feel hurt too. Is this sacrifice? Is this stupidity? Is this love?

Who are you? What am I?

Just when I felt things seemed to make sense between us, I am now perturbed. I don't know how to name it. But tell me, how do you see being away from me? I don't want to hear that you feel the same way I do, because I know you don't. I want to hear what you actually have to say.

What does separation mean to you?

✳ ✳ ✳

HE: (Speaking of Separation)

Speaking of separation, I am reminded of that evening in Kandy hills, when I stood in front of the inexplicable nature that drew its curtains of light. Somehow, that evening out of the blue comes in as an orange memory that marks how separation feels to me. I am bringing back that piece of note that I wrote back then seeing the sinking sun.

Like a heavy heart seeping the pain intensely through its edges, the cloud bore the golden light that spilled the last of its shine on the city. The clouds will miss the lights, even if it is for a brief while, in all the sincerity of their unconditional relationship.

Things we love thrive the best when we give them the space and freedom to be something more; different and individual - a lot like the cloud and the light. In the moments of separation, the clouds shall mourn in darkness for the return of the light; not in tears, but in a silver lining that will light up the souls. And the light shall go around the world to give life to more, showing its fierce yearning in the goodness it gives without asking.

The density of pain is more important than the gravity of happiness.

The distance is more important than the proximity, for in their quintessential ways, they will come together again to make love, as they always do. At the end of the night, the light returns. It hurt good. It meant magic. The fire rises. And the play begins.

Again, in the dawn. I miss you, only to love you more. You are my dusk, and the dawn. All this and more keeps hitting my mind as we endure this distance... how long is art, and how short is life?

Somehow this is how I always felt when I am away from you. I have never been able to put it in words but it took that sunset on the Kandy hills to express how I felt when I miss you. I don't think this is something that arises from within myself but from the love that you shower me with. I don't remember a time when you have not been with me. We had been miles apart on many occasions, but somehow I have never felt the distance that I feel now.

You have always been there for me. I always know that you will be there for me. As much as I have been grateful for that, I have been unmindful of it, too. I have taken you for granted and called it rightful. I have let you wither in loneliness and called it solitude. It has always been about me, and myself.

The side effects of narcissism are often glamorous. That is the problem. We are all in for that glamorous glitch that wouldn't last even a minute. No matter how many times we realize it, we still chase the green paper and the grey buildings. It is so hard to live peacefully in the middle of this cradle called civilization that is constantly rocked by forces of materialism. It is easy to give all the wants up and surrender to the needs.

But why is it so hard to do in reality? May be life was simpler when all we had to worry about were the broken pencils. We had sharpeners for that. There were solutions, and they were simple. The minute the mechanical pencils came, things changed. We wanted more. Sleek and stylish.

We forgot the beauty of the woods even if it meant cutting them down. We loved the plastic pursuits of pleasure and called it passion. We became a product of our environment.

That's how evolution works, and slowly our souls had become a subject too. I realize that now better than ever. I don't wish to go back and change the clock. But I want to live this moment with you like I want to. Somehow I trust love is the only light to all the shadows.

Love is the light. We are its shadows. I feel proud to have fallen for you. You are my light. I am your shadow. Carpe diem!

* * *

SHE: (It's a Brain thing)

You are always about yourself. Everything about you that hurts me, makes me fall more in love with you. One of those notes that I keep close to myself is the one you wrote about 'self'.

'Life is short, but it takes pretty long to realize that. If you have the time to connect, though, it's different. Connections are important. The ones we make with people, things, work and, by large, life itself. But I feel the most important of them all is the connection that we make with our 'self'.

We are all often busy and pour all our energy in connecting with the external attributes of life. Those are essential too, in the world that is dependent on the ecosystem we are building, rather than preserving. But are we really appreciating the actual relationship we have with our self and how important that is?

To establish this quintessential connection, you need to understand what is 'self'.

In my opinion, it is nothing but a collective conscience of everything that you are going through and a clear consequence of all your thoughts and actions. Having said that, it is also the unperturbed child that stays alive in us, not defined by memories or experiences. It is a pure form of noise and music existing separately.

To be able to comprehensively understand self, you have to start with questions. How do you experience pain instead of avoiding it? How do you react to happiness other than getting carried away with joy?

How do you feel love other than the lust that comes with desires and accomplishments? How do you weigh value over skill?

And then, move on to conversations with yourself. Every time you look at the mirror, what do you see? Your face, yes. And the million layers beneath, (not necessarily). But you need to talk to them; relate to them; read them; be aware…

Awareness starts from the mind and manifests itself in the expressions. Only when we express do we get to understand our self, or err or flow. Either way, movement is essential. Start with your body. Utter a word aloud, hear your voice, and feel the way it reverberates through the architecture of your body. Wiggle your toes and tap it to your favourite music, staying lost in the duet that your body and mind have. Jump to defy gravity, even for a second, with all your heart.

Close your eyes, and see. Open your ears, and listen. Look around.

Love. Live. Thrive. Submit. Surrender.

I spent one whole hour of today being with myself, doing most of the above. At the end of the hour, I felt like sharing the same with you. As you read it, every letter in every word, we are touched by the universe at the same time. A beautiful connection of minds is being made between us as I write and you read, and we smile, in the silence of a musical understanding.

Even before we blink, we are in a duet. You are in a duet, with yourself. Inhale and exhale. Move a little, and feel the movement. Smile from the heart. Touch your cheek. Close your eyes. Look into yourself.

How beautiful is this? How beautiful is thy self?

It stirs me every time I read this. It takes me to a faraway island that is too beautiful to be real. This beauty is not scenic, but emotional. It spreads across the mind with all the green and the blue. I feel so happy to read your words, and I am grateful to my functioning brain.

I feel it is all up in the head inside the cerebrum. Everything, including the concept of heart and calling of love, originates from the soft curves of the brain. Even the hardest feelings happen from the fluid zones of the brain. So often we've felt our heart beat, but seldom do we touch and try to feel our brain.

So silent it is. So true.

* * *

HE: (Love halts the brain)

I feel like I am replying to you even before you have finished. That's how most conversations in life are. We don't listen, but rush to answer or impress. Be it sex or chess, winning seems to be the ultimate goal rather than the joy of playing. We always look for the bright and the light, but wisdom lies in the shadows.

Of late, I have been obsessed about the way our brain works. The soft, guarded brain is always called logical, but I feel it is the most magical connect that we have with anything and everything. This very sentence makes sense because of the brain, and it might very well be smiling, feeling this word of acknowledgement even before we know it, because it gave birth to the thought and the next one that follows and so on.

Everything we know, read, contemplate, love, hate, rehearse, hear, feel, sense, segregate, seclude, touch, torch, flirt, flaunt... is an adorned effect of the brain's dream coming true every second. With its restricted access and limitless possibilities, I believe the brain is the window to the universe. It is in our hands to keep it open for love to reach. When it reaches, you wouldn't know it, but feel it. And when it touches, you wouldn't feel it, but know you belong to it.

Mark my words with your eyelids. This is the only time when the sensible and smart brain will falter. It feels a lot like gravity when we fall in love. Natural. Out of the body and brain. It feels out of the universe that we know, like the infinite unknown. It is not manmade.

Love doesn't make sense. It is the universe's calling to express that we are all one endless song sung in different notes of a dream. Can you hear the symphony of the souls connected? It moves to make us stand still.

Love stirs. Love moves. Love is.

* * *

SHE: (Strangers in love)

I feel you have finished faster than usual. Time is another thing that rules everything in this world. I am not a morning person, and I don't remember ever waking up early, except for those times when we would meet up in the beach to wash our faces with the sunrise. Never have I felt a time better than those early mornings that you gifted me. The morning was not the spectacle but witnessing the dawn with you meant a miracle to me.

We used to sit on the sand, our shoulders grazing for the warmth that beat the chillness of the early morning. The skies would change colours constantly. From dark black to dense grey to dreamy pink to descending blue to a definite yellow to a destined mix of colours where the metamorphosis is more than that of a butterfly.

There is no hurry. There are no stop clocks. Slow and steady, everything falls into place. Nature doesn't rush at all, but still makes the most beautiful pieces of art in the blink of our eyes. That high when the first ray of sunlight hits our face through the creek of the cloud is inexplicable. A lot of things in life, especially love, are so.

The irresistible urge to be with you all the time, I somehow feel, is beyond the physical attraction. If I was told years ago that this was only a physical attraction, I probably wouldn't have accepted but still given it a moment to listen. But now that we have come past hundreds of hours of physical intimacy over these years, I believe it is a lot more emotional.

I love how you don't get physically turned on unless you are emotionally invested in the moment, however small it is. You always yearn for an emotional connection. Nothing for you is only physical, even the simple act of drinking water. You always close your eyes when drinking water. Somehow it reminds me of the way you look when you have your orgasm. An intense submission to the moment beyond your conscience.

I feel both magical and pitiful. It is like you form a huge form of me, inside your head. And I wouldn't blame you. I took this on me. I looked into you more than anything else in this life. I yearned for a life with you. I guess I was never worried if I would ever marry you. Marriage was never in the way of our lives. Somehow I knew I'd always be with you. I just knew.

Everyone has his or her passion. For some it is music, for some others it is movies, poetry, or books… But for me, it was you. You are my art. You are the falling star that I caught myself. How to name this? There is no need. The way I am able to put all of my brain into you, sincerely, is a miracle. It is like trying to remember that dream that you never head, when I try to reconcile the parts of me thinking about you always.

I am reminded of those days when we got used to each other. We were more than lovers then. We were strangers. The love between strangers is an unconditional one. There is an invisible sense of ease in being able to let go of each other anytime. That is a different kind of freedom. You can talk about anything, anytime to a stranger, for you'd never meet them again.

Can we be so with someone we know wholly? Can we be strangers in love? I guess we are hitting a rock in the bottom of the pond. A series of ripples are born that travel deep in to the self. I feel this holds an answer, or perhaps a question. What do you think?

✳ ✳ ✳

HE: (The FIRST kiss)

I am thinking of our first kiss now. How did that feel like? I leave it to you to contemplate. I am drawn towards the way it felt as if it happened for the first time, every time. I didn't keep a count, but this kind of kiss happens very often. We'd kiss each other as if it were the first time.

There is a new birth in every kiss. There is the death of time and space every time the lips of loved ones meet. I am now lost in track of time, and all I could see are your lucid lips that await the touch of my love and the breath that warms up. I recollect the note that I had written to you about our first kiss.

'I still remember how I came closer to you, breaking your anticipation, holding you close, cupping your face, and feeling your presence. Our first touch was magical, like a trance that I wasn't able to – didn't want to – come over. Instead, I came closer; close enough for our noses to touch and far enough that our lips missed each other.

In this finite space thrives the language of the lips, holding the words that weren't spoken and the love that was untold. Not that it shouldn't be. It can't be. It felt charming when our breaths met and our lips brushed occasionally.

God, what is there in the way our breaths play? It is so intense and we were yet to know it. I feel hypnotised when I breathe in your breath. It happens when you are so close.

And when I did touch your soft lips and felt you, everything cut loose. All I could think of was the next moment to hold you close and kiss you softly.

Our lips met. We met. Our lips loved. We lived. There was a gentle feeling in the way I kissed you. It is the reflection of the longevity that I had with you, the yearning that I always want to have with you. It is a very different feeling that I am not able to come past. It is like I could taste your entire self in the kiss.

The friction of the touch, the fraction of the second, and the fiction of the yearning. There simply is so much to dream about. Life is beautiful. You are beautiful. I have so much more to say about this. I will. But now, I want to hear from you. Talk to me, will you?

Your voice is the most beautiful kiss I've ever felt'

❊ ❊ ❊

SHE: (THE first kiss)

I have my own memory when it comes to our first kiss. It was past 11PM that day, and we had returned to your place after a long drive. After a few silent minutes that felt like seconds, we made each other's drink and were wondering what to talk inside the newly confined walls that had risen between us.

You made me comfortable with those smiles that reassured me. In a while, you asked me to follow you to the terrace. It was a half-moon, star-lit night. It was the first time I was at your place. You weren't interested in introducing the place to me, nor was I eager to know it. We both were in a different zone of anxiety then, with the waves of emotions that rush from the brain about being right next to the soul that matters the most to us.

I had yearned for the distance to vanish, and when suddenly it did, I could only stay immersed in the moment. So we walked till the edge of the terrace and sat by the wall beside the parapet. There were fully grown coconut trees in the neighbouring compound, and they cast dancing shadows onto us, giving us shelter with their dancing leaves. We didn't have many words to speak, but felt the pressure of proximity overwhelmingly.

I felt like going into my shell, far away, and loving you from a distance that was safe enough to express all of me. I didn't know that such close existence would pause the world for me. I can still hear the breeze, the music of the hustling leaves, and the silence of the skies. The concrete floor seemed like a green lawn, mainly because of the breeze and also because I was with you.

We'd had conversations more intimate than this, but to confront the tangibility of your touch was something else. Our shoulders touched every now and then as we danced to the duet of the coconut tree's leaves. They were in love with the breeze and with themselves. We didn't look eye to eye. I knew you were looking at me, but I just couldn't respond.

The soul that I've admired all my life was blinking at me, and I didn't know what to do with all the love I had inside me. That's the problem in love. You simply wouldn't know what to do with so much love. It chokes you, challenges you, and questions you, relentlessly. Right then, it confused me. I felt ambiguous in a gratifying way, and when I least expected, you held my arm and kissed me on my shoulder. I didn't expect that.

The breeze, the leaves, the shadows... none expected that. A surge of electrical impulses from the shoulder spread over my entire body, making me feel a loss in weight. I was flying, and to a certain extent, evading gravity. I still had not looked at you, and was submerged in the wetness of the kiss that you had placed on my shoulder.

I had been carrying the weight of my family, inferiority complex, immediate debts, intense doubts, and immense mediocrity on my shoulders. That kiss you implanted became a seed in a second, and grew into a tree in the next minute. It was like my brain was feeling all the definitions of love that there was, is, and could ever be.

It was a lot external than it felt internal, only until the first breath after that kiss touched the fragile shoulder that broke into pieces internally. The warmth of your breath… it is a star's source. I don't know how to explain this.

May be I am exaggerating this, but trust me when I say this… I've never melted as much as I did when you placed that kiss on my shoulder and followed up with a breath that explained everything else. Yes, we had made love like the stars would die in our gasps, but that subtle first kiss on my left shoulder remains a feeling that is more than a memory.

Certain moments are so. They just diminish everything else and stand tall, no matter what. Every time we kiss each other, on our lips, a salt of my shoulder always finds its place between our crumbling bodies. Like a scar of happiness, it reminds me of where it all started.

It is a moment of birth.

* * *

HE: (Our first night)

It moves me like music, to think of that night that we spent together. As two souls who yearned for each other, two strangers who were so much in love. The shades of that night stand like paintings made of ice that melt to the music that keeps flowing in. It is fascinating how our brains are wired to each other now, as we converse. I am drawn by the awe of how everything is being realized constantly.

My love for biology comes to the fore as I remember the research I used to do about the human brain, especially after discovering love with you. There are nights when I've cupped my head and cried in joy, thanking my brain for all the sense that it made. Our brain is the most fascinating universe that there is. It is a visionary, and a dreamer. It is interesting to slice into this topic a little more.

Roughly speaking, we have two systems of vision. One prevents us from bumping into things and enables us to move around, hassle free. It is called 'orientation attention'. It operates quickly, saving energy, as the brain is not required to always develop a full understanding of your surroundings. It becomes a muscle memory over time. You are trained to be aware, often. The other system is called 'discover attention'. This operates more slowly, as the brain collects information from our memory to obtain a full understanding of a particular thing or place.

For instance, assume that you are walking down the street. The orientation system allows you to easily move out of the path of other people, and stops you from falling over, or walking into a lamppost. But when your eye catches sight of something interesting, say, in a shop window, you switch over to the discover system automatically to get the full picture. The object you're looking at might seem familiar, but has a different shape or colour. How long you spend looking at the object, depends on how much sense it makes to you, and the number of other things you're thinking about at that time.

We are in control almost always, but how do I explain the lapse of my senses when you sat by my side and I slid on to your shoulder? Neither the orientation nor the discovery took the centre-stage, but a selfless surge of attention that poured on to our brushing shoulders did. 'Carpe Diem' was the state of mind and I really didn't think of anything else. I listened to my instincts.

As much as it felt like instincts, it was counter-intuitive too. It was an organic state of high when I felt both confident and confused. The world of contradictions kept hitting me like a wave that rushed and retreated on the shore of our shoulders. It belonged completely for a second, and beheld from a distance the next second. Trust me, I deeply remember this moment but what was more intense was the way time and space married each other to build up to that moment when I rested my lips on your shoulder.

I remember exactly when I held your hands, looked at those levitated lines crossing paths, felt the skin for the first time up close, and fervently managed to hide the shocking waves that passed through our souls' channels. I kept rubbing your palm to see if the lines would change or the shock would fade, but nothing changed.

Yet, everything changed. In the shadow of the dancing tree leaves and the shelter of the shining stars, we kept talking with our palms. We were smiling, enough to forget the time that slipped through our fingers like water falling through rocks in rivulets. Strangely, when I rubbed your palm, it wasn't just your skin that I felt but the roughness of my skin too.

As a kid I used to play all around the place, and my favourite part of that was hitting the floor. Like falling light, I used to lie down on the earth and scratch a circle around me with bare hands. I did so on concrete floors, tar roads, rainy muds, soft sands, and so on. It just was my thing, to spread my arms like wings and feel the surface around me. My parents said that my hands had hence become so rough, after sharing my softness with everything around.

I felt the other way though. I felt like I took in the hardness of everything around. I felt stronger. It felt true. Somehow I lost that beautiful habit as a part of growing up, and I almost forgot the way it felt to me. Only until that moment when I rubbed my palm on yours… and I had glimpses of how it felt to be on the ground as a child, again.

When I rubbed my palms on yours, and I had glimpses of the way it felt back then… It felt liberating. It felt like I flew high while on the ground. I saw myself lying on the floor and scratching the texture out of the moment. Your warm skin in the cold night stood lit. The next few seconds were magical, as I clasped your fingers gently, and the way our fingers talked is a story by itself. They just had so much to touch and feel and share.

And in a while I had your fingers intact and felt the physical force of love moving me from inside, as I slid myself on to your neck that naturally allowed space for me. I still do not know why I reached out to your shoulder instead of your neck, and that first peck remains the kiss of my lifetime. You had closed eyes and an open mind, and I had moving lips and static roots.

Like a sunflower, I reached out to you for the shine in the midnight and I dissolved unto you. The moment I kissed you, I had closed my eyes too, but could clearly see the way you felt inside, accepting the kiss completely and surrendering to the slide wholeheartedly. You skated your face on mine and reached out to rest your anxiety on my shoulder. I didn't want anything beyond that.

I love us. I respect us. I miss us.

✳ ✳ ✳

SHE: (Love for afternoons)

We talk so much about early mornings and late nights, but seldom about the afternoons. I am an afternoon person. Somehow, I love the afternoons and the warmth they hold. I don't know if warmth is the right word. People call it sultriness. I look at afternoons as a bridge that connect day and night. There is a mood to the morning that rises, and one to the night that falls. It is hard to romanticize afternoons, but when felt, there is a Zen world existing in the afternoons.

Between dawn and dusk, this is about its sheer existence that doesn't lure or sing or dance, but patiently does its duty and stands true to its self. There is something so naked about the afternoons that can not only be felt, but seen too. I've seen that in the silence of the sun overhead. And I was always curious about how people see it too. I spent time in looking what people do in the afternoons.

Actions are our thoughts spoken out loud. When looked at closely, lunch time is the only thing that comes to the table on an afternoon. Few use it to take a quick nap after eating. Few use it to wait for the evening. Few find it boring. Most don't care about it at all. It is like an invisible friend to all of us. 'So what do I do in the afternoons?' I ask myself.

I am transported to my teens, when I used to have a heartfelt head bath, come to my room, close all the doors to make it dark but allow only a warm ray of light to come through the creek in the window that I keep half-closed. I'd let my hair dry in the heat of the afternoon, lie down on the floor, and listen to my favourite songs of the 80s composed by Ilayaraja. Most of his songs enlighten the soul of an afternoon.

I'd just lay there, romanticized by the slowness of the moment, counting the seconds by fingers that would be pulling the chords of my musical mood. Afternoons are musical. Afternoons are magical. It felt tangible – a flood of hormones during these sunny minutes that melted me unconditionally. Ever since my teens, I have yearned for a soul to share this vibe of the afternoon with, soulfully.

And then, like a sky out of the river, you happened. I couldn't ask for anything more but you, who truly appreciated this essence of me. Somehow, all that I wished for was a person who'd truly understand and accept this afternoon person in me. It is not critical to be accepted but I felt it needed to be acknowledged as it is. At times, that is all it takes, an acknowledgement to the trickled series of thoughts. Being accepted gives a sense of confidence that nothing else can give.

I was confident that I could never explain the amount of love I have for afternoons to anyone. If at all I got close to a soul that understands, I'd close my eyes and call it a living-together. And you happened. I keep repeating the kind of revelation you are. We have spoken much about a pure sense of realization that came during that summer afternoon when we made love, like it was the last time we'd see each other again.

No explanations needed but just that sweat of that afternoon and the scent of love, it pretty much screamed out everything that needed to be told. We did go on to have a cup of noodles and a basket of momos. Just like that, the most intense expectation of my life was met, and I didn't have a clue on how justified it was.

✳ ✳ ✳

HE: (The birth of her voice)

The beauty of revelation lies behind that veil. We have been very open to each other, but I still love the things that you have not told me. In a way, they are things that are inside you deeper than I am. I respect and adore that. The unknown is stunning. What if the universe looks at us and wonders just how we do while looking at it?

We are in awe of its trees, waters, mountains, skies and stars, and beyond. The universe might very well be in awe of our faces, flesh, blood, veins, nerves, neurons, and so on. Our body is a universe by itself, full of wonders and magic. If you pay enough attention, you can hear the music of the blood flowing, and feel the rasping of the muscles when we are walking.

What an orchestra our body is! So many feelings and emotions, needless to say, the rush of all of them together when feeling love. An attraction, desire, a destination, a distance... how to define love? That déjà vu is strong. Did we speak about this already, about defining love? But it is different every time. Right now, I feel love is the most essential thing that there is, like in anything and everything.

There is this yearning to live a life that includes all the magic of the universe, where there are no demarcations, like living and non-living things, but only the appreciation for the sheer existence of space that moves and stirs. Right now, as we speak, there might be different universes happening in parallel. There might very well be a parallel universe where you and I exist differently.

There might be suns that ooze chillness, and moons that emit heat. There might be stars looking after us and wondering what makes us humans complicate life so much? There could be flying rivers that laugh at us all the time, bullying for our attention and acknowledgement.

Who knows? Experience is everything, and it takes time to indulge. But we are obsessed with content. We want to keep creating, and feel there is no time. And then, we want to share it with the world. But there's nothing wrong in travelling to the ends of the world, meeting new people in every zone, encountering the beauty and dangers of nature, emancipating the egos in those musical sunrises, losing and gaining our self in parts, speaking to the stars, dancing alone, singing aloud, crying sincerely, laughing madly, riding slowly, walking swiftly, and more... Yet keeping it all to ourselves without shooting a picture or sharing a live video.

What if we don't tell anything at all about experiences to anyone at all? Does it make a difference? I feel it does. And it is liberating in its own way, a sincere way of sanctioning freedom to yourself to create something true and original. It is fine to feel cuffed, for true freedom lies in the limitations that we term as prisons. Often it is the things that we fear or hate that will break us free. Only when you break inside, can you become something else.

Fear is a fuel. Uncertainties are important. I want to miss you more, not because it will gift me more pain or make me more intense. All great creations have borne pain, and have been born out of pain. Our very birth is a painful process. I am not asking for distance to this reason. I want a distance that will let us see each other wholly, including everything that surrounds us. I want us to be a bigger picture.

I want this space so we can begin to get back to the roots of love, which is unexplainable. Space is everything. Not all the spaces need to be filled. Nothing is the source of everything. Emptiness is the gateway to fullness. And for this distance between us, I am not suggesting that we move away or live apart. I want to cultivate this distance between us as we live together. It is like I want to see the whole of you even when I am kissing you up close.

Is it possible? Everything is. I want to have a bird's eye view when I am hugging you. Do I make sense? Does this make sense? Can you hear me when I say this? I hear you, though. I hear the way you sound inside when you speak out. Remember how I would rest my ears on your spine and listen to your voice as you speak? Your voice would be thrumming and reverberating through all the organs and would sound like it is coming from underwater.

I love hearing that. It'd feel immense and intense. I'd keep asking you questions, silly ones to keep you talking, and for me to drop into the depth of it. This is love.

❋ ❋ ❋

SHE: (MORE Conversations about the voice)

It just is present everywhere, isn't it? Love is universal. Love is the universe. It is a matter of space more than time, to let love reach out to you. Like a book, it shall change you for good. When I remember the way you rest your ears on my spine and listen to me speaking, there are many instances that I can recall, but this one flashes across my mind, and I am giving life to that memory.

It was past 1 AM, and I was on the bed, scrolling through my mobile and doing digital window-shopping. You were by the floor, writing the night out of your heart. You always have this fascination for wooden floors when you write. It was raining outside, and the sound of it was spreading in the room sharply.

The rain that hit the trees, the buildings, the floor, the lamp posts, the vehicles, dogs, cats, insects, the silence, structures, and more... it all came together as one resultant music of the universe. Rain is the universe playing its orchestra on the earth. Then came the first thunder. And in a while, when I felt like the second thunder would come by, you climbed up to the bed and hugged me from behind. You then placed your ears on my back, and waited for me to speak. I didn't. I was smiling.

"Are you smiling?" you asked.

"I don't know; you tell me" I said.

"Yes you are. I can hear you smiling."

"Come on, how can you do that? Maybe you can hear laughter, but how can you hear a smile?"

"I kind of did. Laughter erupts visibly, but a smile, it divulges silently and creates a sonata of wellness inside. With my ears on your back, I heard all those musical notes that resonated when you smiled from the inside. One can tangibly feel it if you are close to the person smiling. Not just hear, you can touch, feel, smell, and be held by a person's smile if you are connected deep enough."

"I thought you were keen about my voice, like you always are. And I secretly denied you the pleasure of that noise."

"Why would you call that a noise?"

"If smile is music, I guess anything that breaks it might be noise?"

"And grains... may be, we can call our voices noise and grains, on a normal note. The continuity of thoughts that keep flowing from inside is a pattern that becomes a part of us. We get so used to our voices that they become almost anonymous, like noise and grains. How often do we listen to our own voices?"

"I guess we listen to them when we cry or laugh out loud. Extreme situations bring us closer to our self than any other moments. We are touched, both by the pleasure and the pain of dramatic moments. I guess pain has the upper hand, to really slice into our self and stay longer than pleasure would."

"I think I'd agree to that. In a way, it felt good when you broke my expectation to hear your voice."

"Does it hurt when I break your expectations?"

"Not now, when I want to be broken, so I can be more scattered, wider across, to accommodate the music of your voice in between the pieces of my being."

"But we've been speaking so much already. How does it feel to hear my reverberating voice from inside as I speak?"

"I hope you know it already. It is a penetrating feel, of bare truth making its way after reflecting on the flesh, blood, and the bones out through the skin. Only a part of it has made its way out, the remaining stays inside as stories that the organs say to each other."

"More like the way you feel when you sit down on a wooden floor to write?"

"I wouldn't compare those, but I'd love to contemplate. When I sit on a wooden floor to write, I feel the caress of the tree that has fallen to make the wooden tile possible. I can hear the sound of its leaves falling and the silence of the trunk. I somehow like this state of fighting that the conscience calls upon. And when I write, the letters come alive like the leaves, the words blossom like branches, the sentences appear like the unexpected rain, the paragraphs become the path to the tree that starts coming alive all over again. There is pain in this, but there is also a plausible pleasure of renaissance, though only in thoughts. May be it is real too. A tree might be coming alive in a parallel universe as I sit to write. Maybe all our dreams come true, and it is a matter of time that we realize it."

"I can feel the wood in your voice. And you said the voice that stays inside is of the stories that the organs say to each other. Why would you say that? Like, why not noise and grains like the voices are?"

"I wouldn't say anything is anything other than what it is. At that point, it was relatable to noise and grains. I think everything we see and make sense of in life is relative to that point of time. What felt devastating years ago might feel light as a fallen leaf when we look back years later! Nothing is really static. Everything is accumulated and jockeyed through the time and space. Our voice, for that matter, has been one big discovery that the human soul has made and managed to retain.

Imagine the first words we'd have spoken. They'd have been an unintelligible sound. From there, we've come a long way in picking words and playing with meanings. Our voice is on the verge of our love to communicate. Everything we speak comes as a result of all those efforts that the brain has taken to utter the words, weave them together, and wave them through our body to churn out a meaningful dialogue. We only hear what's being said. The music is always reverberating inside. Our voice is much more than what we think it is for. It is a testimony to everything we've been through and all the wisdom and ignorance that we've hoarded."

"Strangely I was hearing your voice keenly now. We all sound different, and it's due to muscle memory that we identify each other over phones even without seeing each other's faces. Our voices have a face too, and they come without any makeup. They are precious and priceless. I can hear my voice too, as I say all this. The way I sound right now is how a glacier would feel when it melts, or a pond would feel when stirred by a thrown stone. It just is natural, yet unheard or unseen the way it is."

At this moment, you had taken your ears off my back, and rolled over to face me. In the darkness, there was a pristine light. With enough darkness, the lights of the stars and the moon will always find their place to light up a moment of self. It was that moment, and you were looking into my face with starry eyes."

"Are you happy?" I asked.

You said, "I am very happy, especially when doing the window shopping. Mostly, I won't buy. But there is pleasure in scrolling up and down the products' list online. Now... stop laughing! I can see you came in front on a moment of revelation, and asked me a deep question. I don't know... I guess I am so happy that I don't care to go deep into that question. I am careless right now, and there is a sense of freedom to this moment. I think we should buy this coffee table soon. Look at this one, do you like it?"

"We can keep our IKEA online experience for a later time. I'm not talking about the way it feels to you right now, amidst all the carelessness that has taken focus. Of course, it is a luxury to be careless. It feels like a Sunday afternoon to realize the pleasure of carelessness. But I am talking about the way we are together. There are no songs every day to dance to, or roses to pin. In reality, a lot of our life's moments are not dramatic but boring, or should I say, we are enduring. Dreaming to be together is one thing, and living together is a different thing altogether. We've been together for a pretty long time and I am a selfish soul who knows yet refuses to change. So tell me, are you happy?"

It was a long conversation for a night, and by that time, our brains were already wired in. You knew the answer, I'd say. I knew that you knew. But still, it is that moment of reassurance that we always seek. You can call it a lack of confidence, or a need for more confidence; either way, our souls always want reassuring replies. We are all in this line for reassurance, aren't we? So that we can feel secure, safer, and loved. We were tethered to an understanding silence that soon turned too loud to bear."

"Is this a love-moment?"

"It is a lovely moment."

"Because?"

"Because you haven't answered the simplest question I had asked you. You are pretending that you don't care. But the truth is, you do care, and the act you put up as if you don't, is serenely theatrical. I am enjoying this part and my heart claps so loud in joy. Can you hear it? There you are, smiling already, taking a bow."

"Yes, I didn't answer you. There was no need to. What is the fun in a rainbow coming before the rain happens? I loved the slow scheme of things, as a storm of realizations rubbed across our grasses. This is beautiful."

"As I keep carving sense, I am also consciously drawn to the way you sound. Your voice... I just can't get enough out of your voice. It feels sacred to be touched by the voice. All I want to do is listen to you more, like a leaf listening to the breeze with all its veins. In this fearless dark night, as you close your eyes, in the blink of the moment, tell me, what do you see inside?"

"What do I see inside? Well, it has been a stormy night for our clouds. It hasn't rained yet, but in the light of the conversations, I can see a rainbow already. It has lived through the storm and is dancing to the breeze that passes through it. A dancing rainbow in this dark night, you and me feeling its might... How is that for a sight, save the fact I am teary eyed?"

* * *

HE: (The clarity of tears)

That fearless dark night never died. It still lives in our memories, as it is. And towards the end, I was teary eyed too. But perhaps you wouldn't have seen it, for you had tears blocking your vision, or should I say, giving you some time to settle to thinking. In the blur lies the clarity. Every tear is an ocean of salt. Tears are pure. You can laugh for anybody, but to cry for someone takes a lot.

It takes a lot, including breaking the ice in your head, and melting it in the heat of your blood, to spray the fluid thoughts that get distilled in a second, to flood up the throat, hit the nostrils, and reach a point that feels like the exact midpoint of your head. Before you know, a wave of emotions begins from that with a shrunken forehead, skewed eyes and a twisted lip.

And then, you cry. You cry your heart out, and the pace picks up, bringing to the fore all the unspoken words and the compromised situations. The cycle of distillation keeps happening inside. And the priceless tears just cleanse the clouds away, giving the shine that your soul deserves. The head aches, but the heart breathes easy with new blood that has no ice but only the breeze of the existence.

You cry. You let go. You feel light, and appreciate the void in the moment.

I have never felt shy to cry, ever. At times, people have called it my weakness. But I got to realize that it is the vulnerable moments of our life that rip the ego walls apart and bring us close to our self, and to the universe. Of all the tears, it is those that come out of happiness that are even more powerful. Happiness and tears, the contradiction is beautiful. I am ruminating about the moment when I tied that yellow thread around your neck, when we got married.

I didn't believe in the concept of marriage, or the emotions that come attached to the thread called 'Thaali'. But when the Tablas and Nadhaswaram were played in a crescendo, and I was asked to tie that yellow thread around your neck, all the photographers were focusing on you, to see if they could capture a glimpse of your tears climbing down. The brides are always expected to cry, after all.

But their efforts went in vain, as you never cried. But I did. I had tears coming from nowhere. In broad daylight, the photographers later complained that they couldn't get a candid moment of the bride crying. But what about the tears I shed? Were they unnoticed, or ignored? Unnoticed, because, why would anybody expect a guy to cry? And ignored because, it's a shame if a guy cries!

But still, it felt true to me. If you ask me, the most priceless moment of my entire wedding was when I shed those spontaneous tears. I had no control. It was like I had an orgasm in front of thousands of people, yet nobody noticed. Until I told you that I cried so, even you didn't know. It was a divine masturbation. So many times, even you had told me not to cry like a girl. Why reserve the vulnerabilities only to a girl?

Let's accept that there is nothing wrong in crying, and it is only an intense expression of self. What has it got to do with masculinity or femininity? In terms of emotions and values, there is a guy in every girl, and a girl in every guy. If only we could stand up to the fact that fragility and solidity are equally important and beautiful, and it only depends on the individual to express more of either of these according to the situation, there wouldn't be a salt of discrimination or social pressure to be a guy or a girl.

✱ ✱ ✱

SHE: (The liberation in crying)

I have no words to explain how much I love tears. I love to cry more than I like smiling. Yes, especially in my teenage days, I was this soul who loved to find reasons to slip into a sad state and mourn intensely. I'd listen to my favourite song and cry. I'd think about an instance that hurt me in the past, and cry. I'd think of a loss that could possibly happen, and cry. I'd just find any reason that I could, and cry the hell out of it.

I don't know why I did that, but I was into it for the kind of liberation it offered. It felt good. How sad is that? But also, how true is that? I always wanted someone who understood my love for crying. You did. And eventually, of everything and everyone, you are the one for whom I had cried a lot. I am trying to think of the moments that made me cry, with respect to you.

Moments when I felt happy, betrayed, beloved, surprised, together with you, lonely without you... They were lovely moments, but also depressing and desperate moments. The list goes on, but I can't wait to say how much I have truly cried in each of these moments. Especially in those times when you had been close to other souls in your life, even after we fell in love with each other, I simply wasn't able to comprehend it at all.

It is like you were everything to me, but how can someone, anyone, else be anything to you at all, other than me? I know I am sounding silly, given the way I know you by heart. But you know the intensity of my question. It is not like I want to have you all for myself or own you. I do, but I don't think I can or I should. It took a really long time to understand that.

The greatest irony is how a person changes into something else that he/she never saw coming, but in the course of love, it happens so naturally that the very nature of the person stands questioned by self. I wasn't imagining me like this ever, as someone who would accept pain in a way that I do now.

Earlier it was like I wanted to feel pain and cry more. But now, I've become this person who doesn't like pain anymore. It is like I've had enough of this, or I don't want any more of this. I've changed a lot in many other things, too, I see. Reading was my passion and there is not a book that I'd drop without finishing. But now, my attention span is crucified, and anything more than a minute continuously is too taxing for me.

I guess I am not alone in this case. How many of us have the patience to flip through the pages of a book today? We'd scroll through the Instagram feed for hours, but not the pages of a physical book. Physical... How powerful is that word? We claim to be connected always, digitally, but how truly are we connected? In the past, when a guy met a girl, or a guy-guy, or a girl-girl for that matter, two souls used to gaze eye-to-eye.

But today we have a chosen intruder in between, say the iPhone X. The portrait mode is on, and the focus is on the highlights rather than the moment. The compulsive idea that every moment should end in a photograph scares me. It is not always about how long they last, the moments... but the energy with which they occur, right?

In trying to capture a moment, are we missing the moment? In trying to freeze a moment, are we missing the heat of it? Where are we going, and what are we doing? It doesn't mean I am the ideal person to ask all these questions. I am a victim, and the culprit. I have had many situations where I had been lost in the Instagram stories rather than submitting to the moment.

How painful is this?

* * *

HE: (The one-eyed watchman)

Talking about pain brings back so many memories. Certainly we can't recollect and experience the actual pain, but the memories that stay attached to it haunt us more than real pain. An uncontrollable aching wave passes right through the heart, and it is not easy at all. On one side, you want to evade it consciously. And on the other side, you want to sink into it subconsciously.

I guess we are in it, the liberation that pain yields, except for the instances that involve guilt. We are often fine with pain, but guilt is different and hurts more. I am easily filled with a whole lot of guilt than you'd ever know. I have secrets. I hate to say this, but I do have a lot of secrets. You know most of them.

It is not that I wanted to lie to you, but I wished to keep things on an even keel. I hid things from you. And what is it with me and the universe? Every time I hide something big from you, there appears a situation where the truth will reveal itself beautifully? It just literally finds its way home, and even without knocking the door, it helps itself onto the dining table for a fight.

I have hurt you a lot. It is the last thing I wanted to do, but I ended up hurting you so often. It was my nature and I wouldn't blame it on my parents who raised me with nothing but love. May be that is a problem too. So much love on a soul raises the bar on reality, and cuts loose the threads of control. That's only a fraction of the whole part. I attribute the real part of it to myself, and the way I evolved.

It is a crazy thing, to grow up. It is like you have no other choice. A lot of things in life, like maturity, are bound to come when you grow up. As a kid, I used to ask my appa for things like motorbikes, cars, buses, etc. He'd say that once I grew up, I will be getting all those, and I could be on my own. But eventually, as I grew up and got to ride on the vehicles in reality, it didn't really suffice.

In fact, nothing does. All I want to do is go back to my childhood and play. For the love of life, I just want to play. It was in Kalaivanar Street that I resided in Hasthampatty, Salem. It was an area that had a very democratic feeling to it, as in... you will find all kinds of people.

Religion, occupation, age, attitude... it was a mix of many. That's how it was, in every street those days. Back then, say 25 years ago there, I had the best childhood one could ever have. My street had, like... 20 kids, and we came together every evening after school to play. We'd keep playing until our mothers would come out and shout our names. That would be the alarm that we can't turn off. We'd abide for our mothers' sake. We used to play 'hide and seek' as a gang, and the entire street was allowed as hideout.

I'd never forget that particular Saturday afternoon, though. It just remains engraved as a fond memory. Saturday afternoons always felt promising, because we still would have a Sunday to come, and that let us play without worrying about the Monday that followed. As insurance for our minds to spend the moments without any strings attached, that Saturday was livening up.

We were about a set of 15 then, and we had been taking turns to hide and seek. It was around 3 PM when this episode happened. Madhan, the senior member in the gang, was counting until 100, and we were finding our spaces to hide meanwhile, in haste. Madhan always cheated, like he would count just 50 or 60, but would declare the 100 aloud, and open his eyes to come hunting for the hiding kids.

Usually we would hide in pairs, so at the least, we'd have a person to talk with. Nobody likes to be alone. Everyone chose unique, discrete places like the well's bottom, the stranger's house terrace, the auto stand's rear end covered with crotons, the Hindi tuition centre, etc. And there was one particular building, where the smell of freshly baked bread would hit us every time we crossed past it. The square of that street was always lit with freshly baked items, for it was a bakery that functioned upstairs.

But there used to be a huge grill that always remained shut, and there sat a watchman in front of it. He was a simple looking, ordinary, and modest man, except for the fact that he was one eyed. Yes, there were stories about how he lost that eye. Some said that he was a thief who used to climb fences of houses, and once fell down into a cellar with broken steps, damaging his eye. Some others said that he used to smuggle children and when he did, one of the kids had pitched a stone onto his eye, and that cost his eye.

Many such stories e revolved around, and most of them came from mothers to feed their little kids. If they didn't eat well, they were threatened that they'd be handed over to the one eyed man. None of this ever disturbed him, for he was deaf and dumb too. He had his inferiority complexes and naturally was always cold faced, for people used to see him as an outcast or a weird man.

He did look weird. I always used to wonder... How does a one-eyed, deaf and dumb person fit the role of a watchman? Like, what could he possibly protect under any circumstances? He warded off the kids, surely, who used to walk past faster when crossing his line of sight. They considered him a bad omen. But I always took a few seconds to stand and stare at him. Before he would see me, I'd run away.

But on that day, I stood longer than usual, because he wasn't there. The grill gate was open, and it was the inviting smell of ghee biscuits that lured me closer. Also, Madhan was done counting on the parallel road, and had shouted out 100 already. I do not know from where I gathered the confidence, but I actually ran across the street and entered into the open gate and ran straight up the stairs.

Before I could cross the 10th step, a tall figure obstructed my path, holding my right shoulder. I froze and looked up. Yes, it was the one-eyed man. My heart started pounding, and my eyes were fixed on his nose that seemed longer than it had seemed from far. He kept staring at me with his one eye. The moment I started trembling, he took off his hands, noticed me shivering in pain, gave a pat on my shoulder and smiled.

Yes, he smiled from his heart, and that communicated more than words could. He moved aside and asked me to come up with him. I nodded but didn't speak a word. I just stood there, and he naturally held my hands and took me upstairs. Maybe he was able to understand feelings without a language. Signs were his language, and he kept making them as we walked up.

I couldn't make anything from what he said, but I could understand that he was elated unusually. He took me to the central hall, where the bread loaves were cut into slices. Then into the room where the ghee sweets were made, and into another where milk sweets were made. I was introduced as someone close to him in each of the rooms, which I figured out when the people asked me about how I was related to him.

I just kept my mouth shut, but smiled widely. I was given a piece of sweet or bread in every room. I was smiling and enjoying, watching the baking process, and the labour and love involved in it. Back then, it didn't make much sense to me, but I enjoyed the freshness, sweetness, and the innocence of everything happening around me. I can still remember how everyone working inside had a smile despite the sweat that dwindled past their eyes.

I didn't know what time it was, but I could see the darkness that was settling in. The skies were pinkish. He mimed the number 6, and explained that it was late, and we should go down. I began understanding everything he expressed. We walked down, and it was a pretty steep step line. In the second step, I held his hands firmly and started walking down. He looked at me and we just kept walking.

In his hold, I felt a secure thrust. In this silence, I heard a kind of music that dug deep into me as an understanding, or was it the misunderstanding shouting out loud? He paused, and asked me to sit down. We sat in the middle of the steps. And then, something special happened. He started talking to me via signs, and told so many things which I could barely understand. He wasn't trying to make me understand, but was in a spree, telling stories.

They could have been about his family, or his childhood, or the bakery owners, or the kids, or of his one eye… I didn't know, but I listened. I gave him all the attention. After sometime, on his own, he got up again and offered his hand. We walked down, hand in hand. By the time we reached the front grill gate, the set of people who were playing the hide and seek game had already gathered in front, hearing the news that I had gone upstairs.

The kids didn't have the courage to cross the grill, though it was open. They had been talking about what could have possibly happened to me upstairs… was I put into the burning furnace, or were my eyes taken off using hot spoons? Or I was tied and roasted over open flames?

The creativity inside every kid took wings. But seeing me, they were all more surprised than relieved, for I was holding the hands of the dangerous one-eyed man whom the whole street was afraid to look at or talk to. He looked dreadful, and his eyes were scary. He was the most hated person in the area for the kids, after all the stories that their mothers had fed them with.

But everything changed in my mind after those few hours with him. No words were spoken. It was just his presence that guided me through the halls of the bakery-house. It felt warm both on the outside and the inside. Of all the hours that we had been together that evening, it was then when we were standing on the road hands held, that I took my chance to look upon his face wholly.

I looked into his eyes that were wide open, and saw a reflection of myself in the one that worked. I smiled. He smiled, for the first time in the open street. And before I stopped smiling, he smiled wider, and tears rolled down his cheeks too. He cried. In the blink of an eye, he shed tears that rolled down to reach my shirt pocket. The wetness of the fabric sunk into my skin subtly. It was a different feeling.

He simply couldn't accept that the first selfless smile he had got in a long while was about to fade. He didn't stop smiling even after I crossed the road and reached my friends. A lot of this realization hit me in hindsight as I grew up. But it was real and rooted in those few seconds that remained floating between the time I left his hands, and the time I reached the other side of the road.

In these few seconds, I felt a transcending experience as if a part of myself had travelled to the future to this moment where we are here now. And, like a scratch, it felt like time travel as I felt things beyond my age. I felt brittle, born anew, blessed, joyous, heavy, looked after, and beautiful inside.

From the other side of the road, I saw him still waving hands at me, bidding goodbye with tear filled eyes that were full of smiles. Everything changed from then on, even the way people looked at him. There were no more scary stories told about him. Nor any strange stares as people walked past. All it took was a little company for him to realize how loneliness had made him cold, and a little courage for everyone else to see how beautiful he was when he stood there holding a kid's hand and smiling with tears.

That is all it takes, at times… a moment to change everything else forever.

It feels awfully happy and sweetly painful to relive his smile now. I am sure he is out there somewhere, up above, looking at us having this conversation down below. He might very well be smiling with that reflective eye. Can you feel the weight of his vision landing on your chest, with the same wetness of the tear that landed on my pocket back then?

No soul is alone. We are all connected. You and I, we are pretty deeply connected. Neither can we be responsible for that, nor can we blame it! The way a memory hits us, the way we relive the moments, and the way we feel as if we belonged, what is all of this? I still check my pocket every time I wear a shirt. And that tear remains, with a smile.

* * *

SHE: (Watching the one-eyed watchman and you)

I wish I can go back in time and stand in that line of kids who stood opposite to you on the road when you held his hands. In fact, I did stand in that row, in my mind, when I was reading through that moment. I was watching you looking at him, and smiling. There are two things I felt profoundly that I'd like to share here. Let me say the second thing first, for no reason but I feel so.

Secondly, it was the moment of companionship that I saw so intact there. I mean, the one-eyed watchman could have been proud and pretending at instances when people feared him. Fear is the fuel of power. But deep down, he would have felt lonely, and the touch of a kid's presence was all it took for him to realize how beautiful life is. It took a companion to share the joy of life, as it is. It was not like he missed a companion, but he needed one. He indulged when he had one. To make someone happy is the happiest thing ever, on both ends.

I think he felt that, in his own way, and he couldn't let go of that. It is intriguing to feel the resolute freedom of solitude, but once you have realized your own self, and tasted the beauty of emptiness, you need something to spoil it all, and signify the absence of it. Absence is the void that not only liberates, but also yearns for a fill. There is always this yearning, at different points in our life, for the presence of things like joy, pleasure, adventure and a lot more.

Often, it is a fellow soul that brings this all together as an expectation. We believe if we are able to fall in love and live with a soul, then all of these life expectations will be fulfilled. We are wrong. We always come up with this baggage called expectations that is shown to us by the movies and books, not to mention peer comparison, and we fail to see past the entertainment meant in it.

I don't say it is impossible but I only say love can be a lot more than that.

God! Why do I sound so much like you now? Who is it talking, is it you or me? Or the you in me? It is simply hard to differentiate us from each other. At least I feel so, for I am sure you will differ with me on this. I don't know if this is 'two bodies and one soul,' but it just feels like one. Now all of this started from the second thing that I stated.

Want to know the first thing? It is my endless curiosity to see how you looked as a kid. You had shown photographs of your childhood, school days, and all the other phases that followed. But somehow, to be right next to you when you were this kid in the first grade… that was lost in the glitter of a chocolate wrapper… That mattered a lot to me. I had imagined you in a neatly ironed school uniform, but when reading this, I was able to transcend into the careless kid in you, who loved to raise the bars and reach out to people.

You are still the same soul now. Not that you are an extrovert or someone who reaches out spontaneously, but you are this person who intends to speak to the soul inside rather than the image outside. It is always the kid inside that you tend to connect with. I envy that. And I decide to act, as I time travel and become one with the kids there.

So when I was standing there, along with the other kids, I was looking at you. You were that fragile and chubby kid. For a change, I didn't wait until you crossed the road, but took the first step. I reached your side, and looked at you holding that big smile. I took hold of your other hand that waved freely in the air. Along with you, I smiled at the one-eyed watchman. I shared that moment with you genuinely, and it was not about you and I having the same feelings. That was just us looking at life together.

We both had different thoughts of life, but to proudly hold your hands in front of the world meant everything to me. Those 15 kids in front were the world to us. We crossed the street together, and we just didn't stop. We went through the length of the street, as you kept showing all the shops that you were familiar with, and all the houses where you had friends in.

The one-eyed watchman was looking at us walking past, and kept smiling. It meant everything to me, that walk where we had no idea about anything, but lived the present. Both the things that I mentioned pertain to the passion in companionship.

Is this marriage? Is this real? Is this permanent? I don't want to arrive at a logical answer here, for it feels too real to be unreal. I don't want to go past this state of realization even if I am wrong, for I am in love with this moment.

✳ ✳ ✳

HE: (Time Travel)

Everything seemed so perfect when we were kids, despite all the homework and exams. For a second, I wonder, how would it be if we always remained the kids that we were, and just not grow up?

Between then and now - life kept happening. It floats like a helpless butterfly put in a beautiful glass jar. I want to break free. I want to break the jar. I want to be that butterfly. I want to fly high, even if for a day, I want to fly so high that I could see life from afar, and the world by large. Let us assume that I was given immortality as a butterfly, to live on this planet forever, all I would want to do is fly back to the past, however slowly, seeing all the moments I had lived in the while.

I would touch a bit of all of those in my wings, and leave a trace of colour to remember, reaching far back until I get to that day when my father hit me hard with the soft pillow out of his frustration which I misunderstood to be an angry soul's act. Even today, when I recollect the incident, and recite it to him on a lighter note, he refuses to accept, for he almost forgot.

Maybe he is right, that he forgot. Maybe I am still that child who refuses to forget. We have to come to a conclusion on any matter, right? Else, it just feels incomplete. I try to stay focused on the journey I have made as a butterfly to the past, to become that boy on the bed being hit by his dad with a pillow.

I want to become that boy again, so I could endure the pain that was caused, and wait until my dad's anger subsided. I shouldn't have pestered him continuously for a toy car's battery when he was sitting dull-faced with red eyes, after a day that seemed to have sucked the goodness out of him. Life hadn't been fair that day to him I assume. But if only I had kept the calm and been the boy that I usually was, the one who doesn't take anything to the heart, things would have been different. Life would have been different between me and dad.

There simply was a crack that proportionately grew in size and kept us apart. After that incident, we weren't the friends we used to be. But there shall be no lasting regrets, for I am now there again, back in time, not as the crying soul after that incident, but as an understanding soul who opens both the arms and calls appa close for a hug.

Appa cries, comes closer, and says sorry for that momentary flip in his mood. He says that he didn't mean to hurt me intentionally, and expresses what went wrong in his workday. He said he was waiting all these years in the past for me to come to him one day, so he could explain. He had just begun his new business, and something had gone wrong in the process. Something I wouldn't understand if explained. But he did do so sincerely.

I hold hands with him, and walk him out of the room, taking him to the portico to have a view of the street. Looking outside heals the inside. I take him for a walk down the street. I see all the houses, and the one eyed watchman smiling at me in gratitude, even when it was the first time we met. Maybe he became a butterfly too, and touched the moment in the future when we held hands.

Appa was happy and I could feel that in the way he held hands. I do not find this to be fiction, but a version of reality in a parallel universe. And the moment I get to see this vision, my dad will be getting a scratch of this in his subconscious, too. We are now friends, the kind of friends that I always want to be. Maybe it is possible. Maybe everything is.

If we are open like we should be, and talking like we could be, and writing as we do now, nothing is impossible.

Magic is real. This is magic.

✳ ✳ ✳

SHE: (The Story of the Green Chocolate Wrapper)

Being a child is magic. Being a kid is magic. I say that as if they are two different things, but they aren't. I believe the invented words don't change the way our soul strives to be that innocent pure soul which we were born as. Let us stop pretending to be adults, shall we? Look at everything we have built being an adult, and yet we regret having come past our childhood.

We are all but the stories we tell to ourselves and to each other. I am remembering now the story of that school boy and the green coloured chocolate wrapper you had told me. Let me recite it once, for my self to hear now. Almost 25 years ago, the perfection of a morning showed up with a little schoolboy walking the street with his neatly tied shoe laces, the collar crisp like a wafer, his shirt white like snow, the buttons lined up like soldiers on a parade, the belt on line like an angled arrow, and the shorts smart like a slogan!

It was a Wednesday morning, but seemed like a Friday. He walked and walked until he found that little piece of green wrapper on the path. Colours are tempting, all the time. And it's even more tempting when it's a green coloured wrapper on a cement walking path. The world was busy as the 7-year-old kid bent down to give life to his desire.

It was a used chocolate wrapper. Somebody must have enjoyed the ecstasy of opening the chocolate intensely, and tossed the wrapper aside. He took it along and continued walking, adjusting his bag that slid to the left side.

It was not far, his school, and the little boy reached on time. The advantage of an early player did find its space everywhere. For him, it was the seat near the window. Like every logical choice, it did have many reasons behind it. Fresh air, to stay with present during the History class, which was so concerned about the past. A view of the ground with few boys playing then the school bell right in his sight, allowing him to be self-motivated every time the watchman walked past it.

The school bell had rung, and in no time everyone took their places. To save time, the prayer session that had been held in the school grounds till then was shifted into their respective classes. The students had to show their attention for a dozen minutes, as the headlines on the newspaper, thought for the day, and school prayer were recited in a row, by a bunch of students over digital mics, who kept changing roles every week.

The first day's prayer went fairly enough, with a few candid mistakes like the stumble over the transition from headlines to thought for the day, the irregular spacing between lines in school prayer, and the regular signal breaks in speakers. Breaking the routine is bound to gift some chaos. The little boy was holding the green wrapper tight in his hand all the time. It was time to protect it, he thought, as he kept it safe inside his box with so many superman stickers.

The class begun, and the teacher started his ritual of writing on the blackboard. The little boy was smiling more than his usual width. He saw his green wrapper, occasionally opening his box. Two of his friends had already noticed him peeking into his box often, and the curiosity was ablaze very soon. The whole class was talking about it in murmurs.

Eventually, everyone was talking about the green wrapper that the little boy had in his box. Some said it glittered like a star, some said it had popped down from the sky above, and some said it had magical powers. Imaginations are so well constructed during our early ages, aren't they?

The little boy had all the answers, but maintained the pompous act of ownership, to remain silent when asked about. He was looking straight at the board, unmindful of the flutters around. The art of remaining unmindful to the surroundings! That's an interesting phenomenon. Grownups do this too, if you could remember the scene of people standing in ticket counter lines or elevators, looking straight, as if there was no one else around.

Happiness can't hide for a long time, though. It was not a long time later, when he took out the green wrapper, and smiled! The glitter was more on his eyes than on the wrapper. That fragile ruffle, the beauty of an abandoned article, the colour of the careless eyes, the art of envy around, and the science of silence, everything exhibited its colours. Many eyes were on the boy with the green wrapper. He knew he was being noticed.

Getting noticed is one of the biggest pleasures that mankind ever encounters isn't it? How many times have we intentionally tasted the fruit of approval? How many times have we smiled slightly outside and so much inside on a word of appreciation? How many times have we been hurt when we were denied these simple feelings? Crazy math it is, to count these hidden numbers, for they are hidden feelings.

Nobody likes to be confronted. Nobody wants to come out of the world they had built around themselves. So was the little boy with the green wrapper. He wasn't a victim of approval or a slave for recognition, but an intense lover of the green wrapper he had caught recently. He was at peace with 'his' wrapper. Slowly but yes, it had become a part of him. Just like every other thing which we like and grow to love so much, becoming a part of us, no matter what.

That is the price of love – a tint of possession.

Evening came quite soon that day for the little boy, for there were many moments to mark in time. Like the one in the morning when his friend asked him if he could see the wrapper once and was denied, the one in the noon when he showed the green wrapper to all his friends and rejoiced, and the one in the evening when he made an air plane out of the green wrapper to fly all the way home.

The end of school meant joy to all. The little boy had even more to cherish that day. He hopped along, with his heavy bag and light heart, towards home. The day so far has been so good to him. It doesn't happen often, saving the weekends with no school. To be with the thing you love, means everything doesn't it? And celebration is very important, for it is not the minutes but the moments that you remember. He held the green wrapper high in air, and raced with the wind, flying his soul via the plane he had made with the green wrapper.

He celebrated the moment of love.

Can so much happiness be contained in a chocolate wrapper? Yes. No matter how much you love, how long you protect, how far you deny, how happily you share, or how high you fly, you never know what's coming next. What really matters, is being in love with the present, like the little boy on the run. Remember it the next time you see a green wrapper, will you?

It is hard to forget anything at all. We think we forget things as we grow old, but deep inside, everything remains. Nothing really fades. The lies that we've told, the guilty pleasures we've enjoyed, the mistakes that we've made, the souls we've betrayed... we know it all, but try so hard to forget it. Eventually, our mind is accumulated with so many memories that we feel like we've come past it, but the resonance of the memories that we want to forget always make its presence, throughout our life.

If I tell you not to think about an elephant, it's only the elephant that you are thinking about right now, right?

Makes sense? How often are we in this tricky zone of trying to forget things, or suppress even our basic instincts? Repression has become a part of our life, and we strive so much to say NO to our instincts. I wouldn't say instincts are right all the time. But what's the harm in giving it an ear or a shoulder? Whatever we do, are we doing it with a full heart? How deeply do we mean what we say? How mechanical are your 'good morning' and 'bye, bye' greetings to people you meet every day? How true do we stay to our emotions?

The boy with green wrapper does, though. I can still see the glitter in his eyes when he opens up a chocolate wrapper. We are that boy, one way or the other with some chocolate wrapped in our hands. We are not into it for the chocolate, but for the love of unveiling. There is something in the sound of the act that our ears can't hear. There is something in the way it feels that the fingers can't sense. It's got to do something with the inside, doesn't it?

It stirs. It makes you feel belonged. That is what we all want to feel. That's why we indulge in reading a book we love, or watching a movie that connects. We feel belonged when we do that, and we nod faster inside, assuring ourselves that we are not alone in this world. We are company-prone. We want to be in the crowd, even though it frightens us at times. These important moments of assurance become so reassuring, because they are all not attached to the larger picture of life, say jobs or careers or property or wealth, but to the feelings that we emote as basic individual human beings.

I don't know where I am heading with this, but I feel it is all about how true we are to ourselves in the first place, and how sincere we are, to each other. As natural and sincere as that!

Chapter 6.5

The Bigger Picture

"It's beautiful," said the pink star.

"It is," nodded the blue star.

"Tell me what signals are you getting from these souls?"

"You tell me first! I truly want to listen!"

"I asked you first!"

"I asked you firmly!"

"Priority vs intensity?"

"Intensity is the priority."

"I guess that makes sense," pink star acquiesced.

"It has to!"

"I mean, the intensity with which you asked kindled energy in me, even to hear. Exactly what they were talking about too, right?"

"Yup, I guess it is all in the intensity of the moment, and how sincerely we submit to it"

"Totally. Humans talk, write, share, comment, converse, negotiate, shout, cry, and more! They just express so much every day in so many platforms, but how truly they mean their words and thoughts are debatable!"

"Know what? I see more love in the sincerity of a fight that happens between two people, rather than a plastic flirtation that leads nowhere except with the intent to have sex."

"Is it all about sex? And always about sex? Like the urge for every moment to be framed in a picture, does all the love between two souls culminate in sex?"

"No harm in sex, but then, I don't know!"

"Let's debate about this some time, can we? May be including all our friends around. I'd love to have a shine of perspectives!"

"Absolutely."

"So tell me, what are these two getting at?"

"Exactly where we are getting at!"

"And where is that?"

"I don't know."

"I don't know, either. Hence I'm asking you, in the first place!"

"Yet we feel beautiful, why is that?"

"Because it feels so?"

"The power of feelings and the descending space of life in today's world… This concerns me!"

"What are you thinking of now?"

"It is not in the way we think, but the way we feel, that the most precious moments of life are comprehended."

"I feel lucky to have a bigger picture of this. Thanks to the distance, we can see the full picture."

"Yes. Look at them. They started with a fight, then moved onto talking about memories, then random things that mattered more than their personal feelings, and now even more random things…"

"I feel they are travelling back to their roots, to how they found each other, as they were."

"Yes, there wasn't any familiarity at all, but only the love for conversations."

"That's exactly what they are doing now, conversing with only the love to listen to each other."

"Sigh! What a blessing it is, to be heard out without an urge to reply or convince?"

"I am listening to you, truly."

"I am shining more than I would usually do."

"I can see that."

"I can feel you…"

"What do I say now?"

"What do you feel now?"

Chapter 7

The Turning Point

HE: (The duet of the leaves and the breeze)

I sit here now, and think of the way I feel you. I am neither letting my thoughts come in the way, nor making an attempt to move around. Movement is essential, but staying rooted is even more important. I am trying to reduce all the distractions I have in my mind, though they are inspiring. I am trying genuinely to keep them all away. I am getting into a silence that is loud. I am trying to cry myself into that feeling called you.

Even before I know, a surge weight seeps from the extremities of my body and forms a river of realizations and engulfs me. I am gasping for breath, and I love this death experience, even if it is for a few minutes. I don't fear death now; nobody does, until they are close to it. Then what do we fear? We never fear about the past we have crossed, but for the future that we are to go through.

Uncertainty seems to frighten, but it's the most beautiful thing that there ever is. Like the second that just passed, or the one that is about to. It is crazily fast, isn't it? The pace in which life occurs! And the only time where we defy all of this, is when love happens. Hard to comprehend, yet easy to surrender to... You don't fall for something you don't understand, except in the moments of love.

We become vulnerable. We also become veterans. It is in the submission that the beauty of passion lies. Love is crazy. It drives you crazy. But in the end, it makes sense, like a passing bullet reaching its target. You can either catch it, or be caught. It hurts. It liberates. How physical is this? How emotional is this? I am tempted to talk about a memory now, but I am not going to.

What are we, if not for our memories and dreams? We ride on these two... t what is a life without dreams and memories? How about just this day, or hour, or minute? How intense can that be, if we lived every second to the fullest? It needs nothing but our self, and I find nothing more luxurious than that. The moment! Yes, I think it is the moment that matters.

How often do we realize the beauty of a moment? We often forget the beauty of its sheer existence. Anytime, when you stop what you are doing and look around for a moment, you will understand how, beautiful life is happening around. The first time I felt this profoundly was on that evening at the railway station, when I was so frustrated about the delayed train. You know how the Chennai Central railway station is. It comes with a muggy atmosphere, and messed up crowd.

I tried to read a book, but it made me feel sleepy. So I chose to watch the trains go past. I was doing everything to keep myself engaged. Boredom can be cruel. After some time, I closed my book, kept my mobile phone inside my pocket, just stood up and felt my ground for few seconds. I then walked past the sitting passengers, who were waiting for their respective trains. There was no great scenery or simpler peace, but the average chaos of an Indian railway station.

In a while, I felt the strangeness of the events happening around me. I observed. There was a little kid carrying a handful of jackfruit slices, an old lady begging in a decent dress, a weighing machine that was frequented, the empty sight of the tracks without the trains, the rats on the tracks, the noise of the far away vehicles on the road, the people sleeping on the stone benches, the food vendors reciting their routine with a musical lilting, the sound of the distant train's horn…

So much seems to be happening around us, all the time. They weren't extraordinary moments like climbing the peak of a mountain, but felt beautiful as the small moments they were in the journey of climbing the mountain. All it took was my decision to keep my mobile phone in my pocket. As simple as that.

But how powerful did that turn out to be? Not the act, but the addiction I mean, is so staggering. The simple act of keeping an electronic gadget inside our pockets reopens the windows of life, and allows the universe to touch us. Honestly speaking, when was the last time we forgot our mobiles and just stood hooked to the life that happens around us? Think about it. What if all the technology we've ever invented vanishes overnight and we are left with nothing but this wide spread world to take a stroll?

I guess we will come out then, to see how the sun shines and why rain matters. We will have more conversations – meaningful ones at that. To have a real conversation, you have to reveal yourself. You have to shed off the layers that hold you back, and become a part of the flow. We will learn to be alone. Only in solitude can we get close to realize who we are without anything or anyone attached to the conclusion. We shall not be influenced by anything but ourselves.

The word influence is so scary to me. It's an 'influencer' market today. Celebrities act in advertisements, holding table fans, eating noodles, and cleaning toilets. And they ask us to do the same, too. Should we be driven by colours and glitter, or should we be guided by instincts and truth? I am beginning to lose interest in lies, even though they are attractive and far more appealing than the truth.

I feel I will surrender to the truth and become one with nature, as soft as the water that creates, and as hard as the flood that'd destroy.

I come to realize that there is only one flow in the universe, and we are all a part of it. Can you feel the breeze in this thought? Like the way I felt when I was once standing in the kitchen and watching the dancing leaves of trees through the closed glass window. In the silence of the night, I watched the trance of the trees making love to the wind that grew stronger with time. A cyclone was crossing the coast, and its effects were all over the place.

I had the choice to open the door and feel the wind in the balcony, but I stood in the dark, isolated by choice, and contemplated how it would feel to be outside. Even the soul has an inside and an outside, I believe. An inside that enjoys a deeper solitude behind the glass window, and an outside that leads to the inside that precedes the next breezy outside layer. There are so many layers and it just never ends.

There is no mastery of self, as it is the limitless ocean of layers that keeps growing into time and space. But what can be mastered, is one layer at a time – the one you are living right now. There is a beauty in being revealed. How often do you reveal yourself? Not just for a conversation, but also for a real life moment that only you live to yourself.

I guess we are all true to ourselves in that sense. No one closes their nose for their own farts when alone. But one little layer of the outer world added to it, we start pretending and enacting something that we want the world to believe in. Are we the self that we are, or the image that we are building in our social media handles?

As the mind kept asking all these questions and more, I walked forward, opened the balcony door, and stood out there in the open. Before I could see anything at all, the wind hit my face with tenacity. Chennai wasn't used to this kind of breezy nights, and naturally people in and around the city were excited, absorbing the fact that in some other part of the country, this might be even stronger as a storm that affected the peace of the people there.

Another gust hit the face, and I was brought back to the reality, as I saw the trees dancing with its leaves soulfully. I had seen the same sight behind the closed window, but out in the open, it was a different feeling altogether. The clouds were moving from left to right swiftly, and new clouds were taking the place of older ones with rapidity. The moon wasn't visible, but the stars were. I looked at all the shining stars and felt like I was being watched by all of them, or at least a couple of them.

I took the recliner chair and sat back with a view of just the passing clouds. A huge mass of grey in the dark it was, that appeared to become a clean slate one moment, but a fresh mass of confusion the next second. There was a quick lapse of feelings, like a breathless dive into those clouds, or a blind drink out of the green leaves that were vaguely visible even when I wasn't exactly seeing them.

I am seeing them now. They are still dancing. It feels pure to see this dance. No one's watching, but they are in a moment of their lifetime, exhibiting what 'celebration' means. There is a limitless freedom in watching nature at its original pace. It felt beautiful. But is nature not more than that? Beauty is in the eye of the beholder, but what about the nature in its glorious self? What about nature's self?

Yes, it was a kiss from the balcony. But why only stay glued when you can actually step out and make love to nature, too? I did. I opened the door, avoided the elevators, walked down the stairs, found the community door locked, and the security deep asleep.

That resulted in me jumping over the locked gate, taking a walk onto the street that was fully empty, with just the dance of the trees, the beautiful blessing of the dancing leaves felt up close; the hide and seek game of the shadow as I walked through the street lit with the street lights...

I took my time to be one with the light and shadow, realized that I was being watched by no one, submitted myself to the grand orchestra of the night that kept unveiling its colours in silence... and all of a sudden I heard the sound of the Zen chimes hung in my balcony even when I was in the middle of a faraway street. I didn't feel like walking back at all, but I wanted to attend to the calling. I wanted to stand close, and feel the fence of my balcony with the roaming Zen bells in action impulsively.

So I took a walk back, selflessly, from a feeling that I don't want to walk away from. I jumped back over apartment's compound wall. I walked past the security person who was still sleeping like a child. I almost went close to kiss him a good night's sleep but it was morning already. So I climbed up the stairs, opened the closed door of the house, and made my way to sit in the same recliner in the balcony and contemplated all of this.

I looked upon the hanging yellow light. It moved to and fro, like an imaginary pendulum with no rules. The wind gathered force and struck a dialogue with the trees. The rustle of the leaves came alive in a different way, as the sun rose and lit life. The way the breeze touches the leaves – I feel everything stands explained in the act of this, or the art in this?

The leaves and the breeze in a duet - everything about life and love stands reflected in this selfless act. I kept watching the duet they indulged in, and the friendship they shared. I see love in them. I see a legit lust in them. I feel touched.

I am. I can see myself in a mirror's glitch, smiling to myself.

***

SHE: (You are my everything)

You know what? I want to hold your hands and walk away into the woods like we did once, years ago. Strangely, I am unable to remember the date when it happened. But is it necessary? Does it even matter when it happened, for the memory still lives in our minds? How many times have we used the sentence – 'it feels like yesterday'? This truly feels like yesterday.

May be our lives are confined to specific points of realizations, and everything that happens between them are nothing but a day that seems a little more than that. We are born, we get to crawl, we learn to walk, we go to school, we learn to adapt, we study to explore, we evolve to become… it seems like a series of events. But when we fall in love with a person, everything stands questioned and looks stupid, doesn't it?

It is like you don't see it coming. It simply wasn't a part of the plan. Over time, we get to understand the essence of love; that it is a feeling, more than a person or a profession. More than what I can explain, I always felt and understood love in deeper ways through how you have been to me. It is not what you showed me, or tried to adorn me with. It is more of what I felt and realized over time. I want to experience more of it.

I am ready to go far, back into the woods, again. I am ready to experience how it felt when we let go of everything that day, and embarked on a journey into the woods. I was never sure of the kind of person I was – unsure if I liked the beach or the hills, if I am a good or bad person. If there was one thing that I am sure of, it is the way I loved you.

Any time, any day, if you ask me the thing that I am most certain about, I would say it is you. I know I am stupid to say this, but I have not felt anything more joyful than being with you. Does it make me look selfish, foolish, or dependent? I don't know. I don't care. I have no great talents, or mad passions to be obsessed about. All I know is that I found you, and I braved all odds to make sure we are there for each other, forever.

I don't know, they say we all get to witness a miracle in our life. More than you, I guess the way your love changed me into a better person in all fronts – that is the miracle I witnessed up close. It is like catching a falling star and keeping it close to your heart. You are my falling star that I didn't close eyes to wish at, but fell along, in love, with you. I don't know how else to put this across.

I have no inhibitions with you, but why am I feeling so intimidated now? A lot like the way it felt when we made plans for our first ever trip into the woods, I now feel like standing on the verge of jumping into the ocean of second thoughts, though there isn't one.

Chapter 8

Into The Woods

H E: (Growing old with you)

As we speak of the young memories that fail to fade, there is this fascinating conversation that we wrote to each other about our old age, which strikes me now. We weren't committed into a relationship then. We had no idea how our future would be, let alone the idea of you and me being together. But we had each other in us so much that we couldn't really think of letting 'us' go, in the name of marriage.

"Do you love me?"

"Of course, I do!"

"In what way?"

"In every way that there is…"

"Does that mean you will never leave my side?"

"You know you are asking questions that you already know the answers to."

"So what? Just answer me again. Will you always be by my side?"

"Now you have changed the question according to the answer that you want to hear."

"Tell me…"

"Yes I do, I truly want to be by your side all the time. Strangely, I am wondering why we can't be? I mean, we love each other so much and understand our worlds. Keeping aside the physical relationship, what else is barring us from being together? Do love and friendship demarcate themselves just with the border of a physical relationship?"

"I don't think so. Then what is stopping us? Is it everyone around us?"

"Totally. What are the odds of our future life partners, if there is someone else, understanding the way we love each other and letting us thrive?"

"What if they don't allow?"

"What if they allow?"

"That will be fine. But what if they don't allow?"

"That will be grave. What should we do now?"

"We simply can't let go of each other, can we? Even if we do, I don't think anything will change between us. I will always accept anything for your happiness. Your happiness is my happiness. Happiness is us."

"So what does that imply, if we have to part ways for the sake of someone who comes in between? I get that we let go for the time being, and for our life partners. But when do we get to be us, again? This US that defies all the odds and remains the most certain thing in our lives, I want this to last"

"Exactly. We will last. I always wanted to grow old with you. But if that doesn't happen, I want to come over and live with you when we become old. I don't think the society would bar me from coming and holding your hand then. Things are stable when your hands start to tremble with old age. No lust, no second thoughts to be misunderstood. Just the sheer love I have for you.

Think about you and me laughing our toothless faces out with each other. Wouldn't that be lovely?"

✳ ✳ ✳

SHE: (Our first long drive)

We dreamt of living our old ages together. Somehow, it remained a fascinating factor of assertion in our friendship that dwindled between the certainty of the present, and the uncertainty of the future. It doesn't scare me anymore, for we are living together. How lucky are we to have not missed all this youth and going on to smile with each other only ages later? I don't know if we are 'married' now, but I am sure we are living together ever since. Marriage is more than just the social acceptance or our signatures in the registrar's office. It is a deep concept that most of us simultaneously underrate and overrate. It clearly is a league apart, and I am not sure if we have got the full brunt of it yet.

Out of the blue, I am now driven back into that memory in the woods. Ok, I guess it wasn't out of the blue but because you spoke of it already. Every little thing about that trip remains etched in my mind. How old were we then? 24? That's a good age to get lost confidently. We'd have known what it is to be loved, and hurt, by that time. Both of us were busy in our work life then, and were raring to go in our respective fields. We hardly had time to shed. But nothing supersedes the priorities of love! We made time for each other whenever we could. I don't think there is ever a lack of time. It is all about priorities. You end up making time for things that matter to you.

We mattered. We made time. That Wednesday when we decided to leave everything aside, and go on a long drive... how and where to start this beautiful memory? I was standing at the bus stop, waiting for the bus which would take me to you. I was looking at my wristwatch eagerly, trying to go past time that moved so slowly. It was the very same morning when I was complaining to amma about how fast life was going.

Ironically, this wait at the bus stop seemed longer than it actually was. There came the green town bus that almost spilled with crowd. Only that window seat in the second row seemed vacant from the outside. A lot of people boarded the bus before me, but none had taken that window seat. It remained vacant until I walked over and took my seat. There was a transgender woman sitting on that, and naturally the people had avoided sitting nearby.

I gladly moved closer and asked her if I could share the seat. She smiled back, teary eyed. The entire bus's crowd stared for a minute at me taking the seat next to her, and in that second, their meaningless prejudices were broken into pieces. I could almost hear the sound of their conscience breaking. She was my angel who had kept my place. The place was meant to be mine, and I was looking out the window with a smile that I could feel in the face of that person who looked at me with resonance.

She nodded with an understanding. She knew I was going to meet someone special. Angels always know. You know how people look at you when you smile gleefully? That was pretty much it. Unmindful of the many other people in the bus, I was sitting there, beaming at anyone and everyone my face encountered. I then held on to the window bar as the bus moved, and tried balancing by thoughts, the moving scheme of things in my sight.

Everything moved backwards, yet was different from a train window, and

I rewound a little too slowly with the flow. It is a beautiful feeling to see things go backwards. In a train journey it is so fast that a blur comes in and transports you to another world of thought. In a bus, it is relatively slow, yet it gifts a blur in a steady way.

But I couldn't concentrate in the past, as all I could do was wait for the stop where I could get down and cleanse my senses with your face. I was holding onto the cold steel grill. It felt like the chillness of the first time we ever met, even though we knew each other inside out already by then. It was about the way it felt like the first time. I guess we are often faced with that strange beauty of being new to our beloved every now and then amidst the fast moving flow of life.

It was a surprise that you had planned for me, and I know you are not the kind of person who believes in reality. So I was truly curious about what we were going to do. I know we had a plan to go on a long drive, and I know it would be one with nature. We have always enjoyed our long drives. Especially when we had a fight... All it'd take would be a long drive. No big explanations or escalations, just the sheer pleasure of driving through random roads healed us.

It is magical, isn't it, how a simple ride in the car changes the mind over the gear?

A bump on the road jolted the whole bus as everyone belted back to reality. But not me. I was still in the wrap of the future, thinking of how beautiful it will be to have all the time and space for us in the car ride. An unrivaled tension prevailed in the air, and before I knew, the bus stopped. It had stopped many times already, but that stop was different. It was my stop. I somehow knew it subconsciously, and stood up without my knowledge.

Holding together everything that I was, I carried myself out of the bus and headed out to the standing tree. You were standing by its side with a smile. I wasn't sure if it was the breeze or your smile that made me feel lighter. You were leaning on to the white Corolla car, and the parking lights were winking at me. I grinned. I came to you. You shook hands, and gave me a hug. God! Why did that feel so physical? In you and me, it sent waves that felt magical. We've hugged a hundred times before that, every time we met and we bid a goodbye, but that time it just felt different. I knew it. You knew it. But we didn't care to talk about it as we entered the car and settled in with buckled seat belts.

For a while we didn't talk about anything at all. You drove pleasantly as we kept breathing in each other's presence, and pinching ourselves inside to check if it was a dream come true. The first ever long-trip with you, with no agenda but a limitless freedom to be – what more can I ask for?

✳ ✳ ✳

HE: (Seeing the distance)

When you had been boarding the green bus and counting the minutes that were left to reach me, I was standing by the side of the tree and catching the falling leaves. It was a breezy evening. I have seen trees everywhere, but in that early evening, the solo tree seemed so real that it started sharing my feelings. Like every time I needed a pat, it would shed a bunch of leaves onto my head, and every time I needed some music, it would rattle its branches, and break the silence.

I leaned onto its trunk so that my entire body's weight fell to the ground through my crossed legs. I was feeling weightless, and almost felt no gravity as I kept rooting my thoughts in the air. Love was in the air.

Consciously, I was wearing my watch that day, though it didn't work, for I love the sense of balance it offered to my wrist, and particularly to remain timeless and be in sync with the sun. Life was a lot easier when we just listened to the sun. We rose with it and sunk with it. Darkness was appreciated and embraced as it is, allowing our souls to rest.

It still feels a blur, the way you stepped down with all those soft thuds on the ground leading to me, and smiling upfront. It is interesting when two souls know each other for a long time, yet feel like meeting each other for the first time. It was one such moment when you came up close and stood with that smile in your eyes. I knew you were only reciprocating my smile, but trust me; I didn't know I was smiling.

Memories are something, aren't they? Like a river of fleeting moments, it keeps flowing. In a book or a movie, we all love it for the way it is written or portrayed. But in reality, who is going to take into account the pressure that the urban civilization is exerting on the couples to follow the mode of 'life', buy a car, house, and a property more? Where, then, is the peace for the lotus to blossom?

I am resting the drift and coming back to the moment. That moment when you came closer yet stood apart. We hugged, and sensed it coming right from the moment we saw each other then. It felt special and there was no need to talk. We didn't speak a word but walked towards the car with the unison that was close by but still felt like a long way away. You opened the door before me. I had left the car unlocked.

Strangely you didn't shout at me like you usually would. You'd reprimand such a careless act, warranting a corrective action. But not that day. That day was not about perfection, but the freedom to remain careless. It felt different. The next thing I remember is that, I was driving the car and you were driving me crazy with that look of yours landing on me. I felt the weight of it. Tangibly.

After crossing a mile, you uttered the first word to save me from the silence that drowned me in anxiety.

"So?" you said in a perplexed tone.

"You tell me…" I asked in a tense tone.

"Does it have to be the lady first always?"

"I don't think so."

"What do you think, then?"

"I don't know, just this magical happening… I mean, this is not a surprise, for we planned to meet. Why does it feel so new and free, as if we broke from the shackles?"

"Our lives typically fall into a repetitive routine, often breeding contempt. But take the case of two souls in love. They have so much happening between them emotionally every day. It feels so new every time. But when they face the same feelings every day, what does that reflect? Will it breed contempt?

"It need not, necessarily. Even the taste of contempt will result in something new, like a fight that will rekindle the memories and stay lit.

It is upon the souls to attend to this calling or carry on with the noise of routine."

"Routine is such a dangerous thing. If there is one thing that I can ask the gods to banish from this universe, it would be the seemingly entertaining routine that people are attracted to, with nothing but the temporary yield of fun. What I am interested in is happiness, which is far more than fun!"

"Where are you going now?"

"I am not going to say."

"Where are we going now?"

"I don't know!"

"I'm loving the differential meaning in the questions and answers."

"It does add up to make sense, in the way that everything we ever need is always within us, be it emotional or physical."

"So you are not going to say where we are going?"

"Like I said, I don't know. Maybe I know, but am not certain yet."

"That's enough confusion. Honestly, I don't care, either. It feels like a dream, this drive, and watching all the trees run backwards, slow and steady."

"What do you feel?"

"That's a profound question. But luckily, I am not going to have to think a lot to answer that, for we are driving away from the city. This means everything to me. The traffic is fading, and so are the horns!"

"I feel one with this silence. Maybe this is our birth right, the silence that we experienced all the years along inside the womb."

Just when I was to shift a gear, you had placed your hands on the handle and I rested mine on yours. We stopped talking. Somehow, everything stood translated in the friction of our fingers that held to each other firmly. There was a language that seeped between the fingers, yearning to be filled unto each other. I kept smiling with every gear shift, which I did more times than was necessary, and I am sure you were smiling, too.

I could feel it in the fragility of your fingers that rose every time I held them a little closer during the shift. We were completely into each other, yet not acknowledging an inch of space that stayed lit. Strangely, in the far outskirts, there came a relatively crowded town that demanded the car to slow down.

✳ ✳ ✳

SHE: (GOING THE DISTANCE)

It was a crowded suburb, and people were crossing the roads. Usually, we would let go of each other in a crowd, whatever hold that we are in. But that day was a different note. You didn't let go off my hands in spite of a dozen people staring at us. I guess it is so obvious on the faces when two souls are in love, from their gleeful smiles and crazy actions.

I felt people knew about us, and how crazy we are about each other. I felt like a painting being viewed by everyone around, but I felt proud at that moment, rightfully without shying away. You were always the first to retreat, but you held my hands firmly then, as we waited for the pedestrians to pass by. You then drove past the road that slowly disappeared. And the natural space emerged again.

There is a peculiar kind of joy in getting past the concrete, and crawling on the greens. There were green pastures all the way, and farmers doing their routine under the sun. You didn't shift gears, but I held your fingers a little tighter as I had this exhilarating feeling. We kept passing many green agricultural lands, with people like insects placed between them. I guess we travelled long, but it felt very short.

A lot like art, a lot like life. It was like travelling into the future, and I was having glimpses of it even before it happened. Déjà vu is different, as you feel like you are passing through something that had happened already. But this was even more different, as I felt familiar with future. I felt absolutely normal even with this super power, and I guess all that was there was the hold between our fingers.

Can the friendship between the fingers be so intense? It was much more than I ever imagined. I was having glimpses of us sitting by a waterfall and holding each other. True or not, such dreams have to be treasured.

Not all dreams get to be realized. Not everyone discovers their purpose. I am glad I found mine. I am glad I found you. I don't know what else to say. I am this idiotic, hopeless soul that loves you, and only you.

But what is it that makes me so madly, truly be in love with you? I am not talking about falling in love, but about being in love. I did fall for you, I agree, but what is more important is this moment when I was rising with you. I sensed that you were slowing the car, and nothing can replace the panic I felt about our journey coming to an end.

I honestly wasn't concerned about the destination. A destination stops us. Will it ever give back a mile of the journey or the wait that happened for the crossing sheep herd? Can its loudness ever compensate for the quiet moments encountered in between? I don't think so.

It was intriguing, how we sat in our seats as if we were standing on our feet. I stopped the car, but we still moved. There was palpable tension in the air. We still had our hands glued to the gear lever, and took it off consciously, yet acting as if it had happened naturally. Our hands were wet with the moisture of each other's fingers, which we realized only after the cool breeze hit us partly.

You opened the door and stepped out. Before I could react, you were there opening my door. I stepped out too, in the falling sun that had its vigour. I could see that we were far away from the city, as there were absolutely no horns or buildings around. It was a green spread of grass that led into a thick mass of trees ahead. I was standing and staring into the green space as you were picking up stuff from the back seat.

I hadn't brought anything at all, other than my curiosity about how this evening would be. I was standing there, with my eyes closed for a brief while, and only feeling the breeze hitting me. The rustling sounds caught my attention, and I was picturing the leaves and the breeze in action. The flutter, it intrigues me. Somehow everything that there is, seems to become evident in the dance of the leaf and the breeze.

A leaf is an essential being on the Earth that carries life, and breathes life. A breeze is a tangible form of magic that the soul can embrace. When they meet each other, there happens the duet, intense love being made between the breathing leaf and the blowing wind. There is freedom, there is a force, and there is fragility. Most importantly, there is a flow of life in an infinite cycle. It keeps happening, as long as it is meant to.

And then, the leaf rests; the breeze sighs. There is a calm.

More like the silence after making love, they rest, only to catch up with each other again. The breeze kisses, the leaves flutter, and love begins. Love never ends. It always begins. You closed my door with a thud, and I opened my eyes to came back to the ground that held us patiently. We walked a few steps further, and stared at the wide-open view ahead. It was green everywhere.

About two kilometres ahead, trees were dancing tall and loud, the sound reaching us as muffled piano key presses. I truly wanted to break the distance and get closer to nature's act of love, and watch the wildness of nature up close. As if you heard my thoughts, you held my hands and walked in front of me. That was a magical sight, to have you in front, leading the way. I had always wanted this. I had always wanted my guy to lead me. There is a pleasure in being led, and submitting completely to the direction.

I usually am not the person who likes to be controlled, but that time, I wanted to. It felt progressive in a strange way, as you kept walking in that long green grassland. We kept walking in silence that was better understood than words. It just felt cosmic and comfortable. And did I mention that my entire body and soul was heaped onto that holding hand of yours? We were getting closer to the trees I thought, as the sound of the hustling grew louder.

But it was a long way ahead still to cross the grass scape. By then we were walking shoulder to shoulder, equally, and you had given up the lead. I sincerely didn't know when we would stop the walk, and didn't care, either. Just the brushing sound of our legs on the long grown grass needles as company, we kept walking as if we knew where we were headed. In this azure spirit, there came a time when we halted on the horizon's end. It looked like a proper forest with a thriving sense of life in front. I didn't know it until then, but like I said, who cared?

"Is this a forest?" I asked.

"It feels so," you said.

"Now don't tell me that you don't know what lies ahead?"

"Well…"

"Don't answer."

"Let me finish what I wanted to say…"

"I guess there is no need to talk. Let's walk!"

You dominated. I surrendered. We stood our ground, smiled together, and looked forward to all those trees that seemed to understand. How expensive is an understanding? How pitiful is that we always relate a moment to its worth? I don't know. We are used to this. At least, I am used to this. Like anything and everything we do, it has to be attached to an outcome.

What will it yield us? What benefit will we get? Both questions make the same sense, but then, they never end, do they? Our desires, I mean. But that moment then wasn't falling under this price tag. It was when we were far away from life that we were used to. Anything new is a challenge but also an adventure. It gives us the opportunity to be what we want to be.

For instance, imagine the scenario when you are joining a new firm. Everybody in that firm will see you as you are there. Nobody will know whether you are an introvert or an extrovert… they will accept you as you are to them; as simple as that. So what does this gift you? A chance to be a new you! If you want to be more outward in your conversations, go ahead and talk to folks. If you want to be more creative, come up with crazy perspectives. You will be seen as the person you are, and eventually become that person.

How convenient and powerful is that? Right then, holding your hands, I was in such a free zone when all I cared was to be in love. I was in love. We were in love. Everything above happened in a whirl of a second, like between the second that a leaf fell from its branch to the ground. High on love, we took our feet past that moment.

Nothing is original, but that moment felt new to me, because otherwise, everything is a copy of a copy, of a copy. Even our very existence involves the influence of so many generations that had traded genes through centuries. Our forefathers, and foremothers, had left enough residue of memories in us that we are subconsciously attached to what they are. Nothing is original. Nobody is unique. But what stands out are the rare moments of freshness when we feel separated, unique from our genes, memories, and experiences. What can I say? I wouldn't say I was happy. I've said this already, and will keep saying it. Happiness will never yield anything new. May be a settled satisfaction, yes. But where is the fun in settling down? Only when you are sad will you be frustrated, only when you are frustrated will you be agitated, only when you are agitated will you be disturbed, only when you are disturbed will you be moved.

That is all it takes! Movement is essential, and a superpower. If you look close, everything becomes a memory or a dream, but this second that passes through my hands and your eyes is magical. It doesn't confine to any rule. It doesn't ask for any record.

Irritation is the inspiration. I was in a jinx of all these, and ultimately, felt excited to keep walking. It was a joy more than happiness, and solitude larger than sadness. One step at a time, we kept walking into the messy bush of plants that were tall enough to be trees, but soft enough to be plants. In a while, we entered a free zone where the rustling of the leaves stopped. Right then, it was an array of tall trees that seemed to be welcoming. I wasn't sure of what variety they were.

It is beguiling to wonder how these trees live all on their own, with no tendering. I mean there is no caretaker to this mass of trees, or anything that lies ahead. How come everything thrives better here than any other fostered garden in the city? I guess that is the nature of nature. Nature is everything. We only have to let it be.

I let us be. The setting sun was peeking through the gaps, and we kept feeling its kiss every now and then through the dancing leaves. The breeze was intact. I peeped into the thick solid wood that looked new to be. Everything looked new to me. You were more fascinated with walking through sheer nature. Who doesn't love nature? If only we are bitten by the fangs of nature, we would never really want to return to the routine life that demands plastic diplomacy. Gifted are the souls that wander through nature. Animals are gifted. We were gifted.

It was supposedly the kind of place where anyone would want to stop and stare at those sky scraping trees dancing beautifully to a strong wind. But we didn't stop walking. We didn't start talking, either. Even when I thought we should stop and stare at the splendour in action, the force in your foot forward took me through the frozen seconds. We somehow wanted to move. And it wasn't to reach anywhere, but just to move forward.

It strangely felt like morning all of a sudden with the dawn chorus of the birds coming in and the shine of the sun playing games. The mild hissing of the trees kept filling our ears, and they didn't seem tired in any way. Like I said, it felt like the fresh morning right then. We lost track of reality and found home in the thoughts that hooked us together. It felt as if we were time travelling, moving past the days, months, and years that kept us separated, needing marriage for the society to validate us living together.

What difference does it make anyway? I don't know.

But our very culture is rooted to the act of marriage, isn't it? In fact, marriage is the only place where all our rituals take centre stage. When else do we worship fire passionately or seek blessing sincerely, or invite people generously? I never believed in marriage. You did not, either. But what made us fall victim to the situation that we yearned for it? Maybe because we loved our parents so much. Or they were too afraid of our relatives or the society... Or maybe, because it wasn't a bad idea after all, for the goodness it brings in.

All these went past us, as we kept walking. It was like seeing the world go back in a whirl from the window of a moving train. We were perspiring, not because of the physical exhaustion, but because of the mental miles we kept crossing. The desperation to go past all this and live together forever stood translated in our breaths, which constantly kept speaking a language in our every sigh.

A flash of light sharper than the sunshine pierced through the leaves, followed by thunder that rumbled far away. Before the next clap of thunder, we reached the end of that stretch of trees, and we were standing on the edge of a land that began to slide down. Wide open with shrubs instead of trees, what enthralled both of us was the waterfall visible in the far corner of our view in front.

The falling water gave rise to ascending vapour, and almost created a rainbow, were it not for the Sun that was covered by the clouds. I instantly reached out to my phone to check the time but I remembered leaving it back in the car. I saw that you weren't wearing a watch, either. No mobiles. No watches. Just the sheer brilliance of nature to submit to! What can I say?

✳ ✳ ✳

HE (Looking at you)

We were literally feeling lost. I don't remember the last time I reached a place without Google Maps. But this place looked out of the world. We did sit by the edge for a while, and rest our legs. It was almost like a mudslide that would lead us to the next territory, and we sat down. We left our legs suspended in the little mass of mud hill that let us have this unforgettable view. There was a kilometre in front, but that particular view of the living waterfall killed the distance.

We tried to focus. Focus is everything, isn't it? In a world where we are constantly distracted, people who are able to focus are rare gems. Even when I sit to write, there is this process of reducing all the hanging thoughts and keeping the slate clean for the words to appear. In the process of cleaning the mind palace, I do allow certain distractions to stay behind. I'll tell you why.

When we are distracted we lose focus, and our minds go on a trip to places where we did not intend to go. So we are taken far from where we are. And in a while, when we are done with the trip, when we look back to our source, it appears whole and more beautiful. This distance gives a perspective, and allows us to approach our intentions in an attractive way.

Distance is the inspiration, and the key. And it all depends on what kind of distractions we allow to stay with us. This was one hell of a distraction, I'd say, to sit and watch the waterfall from far and slip into a conversation.

"How beautiful is that?" I asked.

"Beautiful!" you stated.

"I understand. There is no need for a superlative here. Nature needs no adjectives."

"Neither does love."

"I don't know how long we were walking together, without speaking to each other. It feels like we've been conversing all the way along."

"That's because we did. Not through words but by the mere holding of hands, we spoke all that there was to say. I did hear you, like you heard me."

"I am looking at my hands now, and feeling the ink of times crossing the lines."

"Forget not the space between them, the ones that only you can fill..."

"I love being this romantic... who values this moment more than anything else."

"I love being this hopeless romantic who values you more than anything else!"

"What do you see now, apart from the waterfall in the glow of the setting sun?"

"I see a rising love through the path that will take us to the waterfall. Shall we walk?"

"And talk?"

"Of course."

"Loving the certainty,"

"And the uncertainty!"

"Say it!"

"You know it..."

"I mean it..."

"I mean it, too!"

You gave yourself a push to stand up on your feet, tapped the sand from your back and offered your hand for me to get up. Instead of taking your hand, I kept looking at you from the ground. I have always opened the doors for you in cars and restaurants, because it felt good to me to have you at ease. Also primarily because it has been jockeyed through the ages that the guy always opens the door for his girl.

Right then, it crossed all this and felt so true on how it felt to be offered a helping hand. I was a little lost in the moment and kept watching you still, as you nodded gestured at me to hold your hands and get up for the walk ahead. I was wondering what kind of background music had been playing in my mind then. There is always a background music playing in our head for every occasion. Life is interesting that way.

But strangely, from the moment we closed our car doors until that moment when you were standing with your hand extended, there had been no background music, save that of the wind jeering the trees and its leaves. Inches apart, our universes were waiting to be synced in the hold of our hands, again. I took my time and smiled at you, like a wide beam of morning light. You slanted your head to the side and smiled with an angle that your whole body aligned to.

Suddenly, everything around sounded sharper to me, and my vision was clearer too. The red sand around had let out the heat accumulated from the day to everything around, including me. The green trees that were looking characteristic with a unique dance, the orange skies that were bleeding yellow, my white shoes that were brown, your black hair that flew with the breeze to and fro like the blue sea... the colours became so vivid that I went into a trance, and in the split second, you took your hand back and kept smiling at me with the wonder.

You were with me that very second, and we were understanding each other just by the sight of each other. You eclipsed the sun behind you, and shed a smile that overpowered the silhouette and showered a light that touched me. Without me doing it, my hand reached out to you. You walked a step back and smiled in symphony. It felt musical, so musical, this silent smile that held us in its arms. You then came forward and held my hands.

Feeling the force and the fragility, in a wink, I got up and tapped the sand off my back. I still kept smiling, and so did you. We were walking past the red sand, which kept watching us along with the green trees and the red sky. The sound of our walk was muffled into space as we moved forward. Of everything, the red sand kept looking at us, with our imprint on it. My hands were printed on the sand. So were yours, from when you were resting at ease with grounded palms and risen eyes towards the setting sun.

The imprint of our features on the sand would stay there forever as long as it takes. How am I to explain how magical it is to submit to the eye of the red sand that kept seeing us fade into the greens? How many times have I used the word magic already? And I know I am going to be redundant.

You are magic. Is magic real?

You are real. Magic is real.

✳ ✳ ✳

SHE: (Love and laughter)

I still feel the weight of your body resting on to my palms as I pulled you up. I am generally not capable of lifting you, but back then I did. Was it my strength, or your fragility? Either way I felt gifted and powerful to be able to lift you into my world as we moved forward. The sound of our feet brushing past the sandy earth was so rich. I felt rich. I am not a materialistic person, but I love the comfort that things bring in to life. I know you are just the opposite and it was fine with me. Neither you nor I complained anything about each other.

Acceptance is a different kind of pleasure. Besting any other gem on earth, I felt rich in the possession of a state of mind that felt exceedingly wealthy. We kept walking through the whispering shrubs for a long time. The skin of the inner palm, the fascism of the fingers, the intrusion of the sweat, and the invasion of the breeze – there is so much in the way we hold the hands of our loved ones. We kept walking, and talking.

"What is going on in your mind now?" you asked.

"You sound like Facebook," I said with a smile. You laughed out loud too.

"Well, there are no network towers here. And we don't have our mobile phones either. Just forget about the attention seeking avenues, and truly share with me, what do you like about this walk?" There was an insistence.

"That's two questions in a row. What should I answer first?"

"Go in order, will you? Order is easy, at times."

"What's running in my mind? I don't know. I am not thinking of anything."

"But you ought to. Something must be running in your mind always... Should it not?"

"Not necessarily."

"I know; you have said this to me so many times. In fact, one usual question from my side every time we meet would be this."

"What are you thinking about now?"

"Yes. Exactly. That would be my question to you!"

"Now answer me. I just asked you the same. What are you thinking about now?"

"I am usually prone to thoughts. But this time, I am blank, with nothing but the awe of the moment. It feels like a dream to me..."

"I am not going to talk about this. For the first time, I am feeling something that is out of the world even though we are grounded here. I don't know about anything that lies ahead but I trust you in this hold. I can come any distance with you. Cross any river or mountain. You know I will do anything for you, don't you?"

"I know."

"What do you know?"

"That you love me so much."

"And more..."

"And more!"

"So is that what you are thinking now?"

"You want an answer, right? But I don't have one. I am feeling numb. I have nothing to say, but so much to experience!"

"Experience is true luxury."

"And I am rich."

"We are rich."

"I think you always were. With the kind of mind set you have, you are a wealthy soul!"

"You are, too, with the way you love me. To be loved is the most beautiful feeling there is. You gift me that abundantly."

"Do you ever get fed up with me?"

"For?"

"The sake of it."

"For the love of you, yes. For the sake of it, no. I never take you for granted."

"Are you sure?"

"Wait, I think I do at times. That's the consequence of a love that grew from obsessive roots. It is like... you know the other person is always there, and you start taking them for granted. I feel I have done that a lot with you, but instead of feeling like a culprit, I feel like the victim now? Why is that?"

"Because you love me,"

"And?"

"You love me so much, that you are the good in the evil..."

"Why speak about evil?"

"Why not? It is perfectly fine. We are all evil. I am evil. Let's not drive that fact away from the proposition. A little evil is necessary for us to appreciate all the good that we are blessed with feeling."

"If you say so..."

"You need not accept wholly!"

"I didn't, either. Or rather... I couldn't!"

"That's understandable."

I had a very funny walk, and you had a funny run. Till then, we didn't have the chance of witnessing it to the fullest. But yet, in glimpses we did. I saw you walking in a zigzag pattern like always, and I wanted some distance to see it patiently. I left your hands without notice and asked you to walk forward. You did, but there was nothing funny about it. I asked if you could run for me. You stood bewildered, beside a bush.

"Ask me again?" you said.

"I want you to run for me," I repeated.

"I will, if only you will walk for me. I love watching you walk."

Without a word further, I started walking in front of you like I always did. You smiled and started running backwards, with your back facing the unknown behind. We kept looking at each other's embarrassing acts. How lovely was that? It was real fun to see each other in our vulnerable positions. You were running crazy, and I was strangely not worried if you would stumble. I knew you would do just fine, until that moment when you hit a stone and tumbled on the green masses.

I was taken aback, and ran towards you with a morbid look on my face. You were there, with your shoulder against a trunk already, and I was looking to see if you are all right. You gathered yourself up, dusted your elbows and pants. You bled on your right arm that spilt its spread on your blue jean as you rubbed across.

"Red blood, Blue jean and the green leaves around, what a combination of colours," I said, looking at your face.

"Indeed, indeed!" you agreed restlessly.

I laughed. You laughed. I sat on the ground and started laughing out loud, for all good reasons. You joined me in a while. With no reasons or motive, there we were, in the corner of a teeming forest that seemed to be in sync with this. We kept laughing, sitting on the sand and pushing each other to the sides, gaining imbalance. You were the first to fall on the ground. With a soft thud, you fell onto the ground and gave up even the little resistance to stay up. The hysterical series of laughter continued and our cheeks and stomachs ached.

Chapter 8.5

Almost There

"These both I say," said the blue star, with its feminine laugh.

"They are so much in love," nodded the pink star, with its masculine smile.

"I am finding it hard to differentiate who's who now!"

"Exactly. A lot of times, I had to pause and wonder if it's him or her talking"

"But that doesn't matter, I guess. Sharing matters, and they are doing it wholeheartedly!"

"Maybe this is what they call two souls becoming one."

"Maybe,"

"What's going to happen after this?"

"I truly can't wait to see them walk past the next little stretch of land, and how they would be changed forever!"

"That's how it is, the most defining moment of our life always lies just around the corner. It hits us when we least expect it. All we have to do is take the extra yard or metre. Forget a mile, every metre matters. You never know what awaits you."

The stars had seen this already when it actually happened. They know this memory. But every time a powerful memory is relived and retold, it rejuvenates the souls again and kindles a kind of spirit that only stars can create. The amount of warmth and the light happening inside the souls are equivalent and exceeds those of the stars at times.

Chapter 9

Wild Love

HE: (Crossing the long tree)

We were on our feet. With a huge sigh, we walked in front with a relieved leg. It had been a long time since I laughed out like that. I wondered if I was capable of laughing so much. Moments like these remind you of whom you really are, show you the inner kid, and encourage you to run back to it. The truth is, the kid is not in the past but right here with you. It is about the connecting to that and staying with it.

Does that mean one should not mature? I don't think so. Maturity in the mind has to be there. The kid also has to thrive. Ah, that's a tough and thin line to balance. I guess I let go off the balance long ago, and have been leaning towards the kid-side all the time. Most often, I don't have a matured mind like you do. I don't say this to escape from my responsibilities, which I do to a certain extent. I am trying to be as open as I can be to you.

The terrain ahead looked like it was coming to an end. That was the first time I was walking into a forest. Strangely, till date, you had not asked me how I found that place, or was I there before... I guess our best memories remain like that, hidden deep and safe, with a constrained freedom of coming alive anytime. Like it is coming alive now, as we walked forth.

You were watching the plants and trees on your sides, and I was watching you. I love watching you when you are not aware of it. I see a different person in you then. I lost track of everything I knew about you, and was looking at you like I was doing for the first time. Your eyes and hair and skin, everything seemed new to me. You halted and looked at me.

"What?" I asked.

"The tree," you said.

"What about the tree?"

"There is a tree here in front of us. It looks tricky... How are we to cross this stretch?"

Except for that tree which had a large branch jutting out, the entire stretch was a veil of thick bushes that didn't look penetrable. It was like a fort of foliage, being guarded for good. Nothing could be seen past that.

Not a streak of space to sneak peek through, no.

"I guess this tree is our only road across this green fort. Can we hop on and climb through it?" I asked, with surprising clarity.

"But I have never climbed trees so far. And I am sure you have not, either," you said and kept assessing the other options.

"Remember the only thing that I told you before we started this trip?"

"Of course. No matter what, we are scaling the entire stretch for this walk. We shall not stop until we want to."

"And…"

"Wait, I am not asking for us to stop. I am only thinking how to get past this. You know what? Let us climb this tree!"

"Yes, there's a first time for everything."

We dusted our hands with the mud beneath our feet, and got ready for the adventure. There was one strong branch of a tree that extended, seeking sunshine. This was the only possible way to cross to the other side. The green thorn bushes were tall and thick as a mass of army guarding the forest that laid ahead. Security is mandatory these days. I have always wondered why even the most powerful gods have locked doors in the temples.

Up you jumped, even before I could make a move. You reached out to calculate the height of the branch, but there was no need, for it was reachable from where we stood. Then I realized it was reachable for me only. A 6-foot-tall stature has its advantages. I came forward and pushed the branch down for you to climb. It wasn't as tough as it seemed, as you hopped on to cling to the branch.

When was the last time we crawled? As a kid or in an outdoor activity, but other than that, we don't often crawl do we? We had to, this time. I followed your lead as we crawled like snakes that were learning their ropes on a tree. It felt supreme to actually do something we were not used to doing, especially to cross an obstacle. We struggled our way through as we held on to the branch, and your legs were right on my face as you kept kicking your way forward. It was a new experience.

Good or bad, every time we have a new experience, we stand changed. Crushing our bodies through the thick branch that had seen many years of light and shadow, we finally reached the trunk that seemed large enough to accommodate both of us. Every tree trunk is different. Some are sleek. Some are large. Some are strangled. This one was just perfect for both of us to step on and slide down to the ground.

You landed and raised your hands to celebrate, as I slipped a little seeing your joy and landed roughly. You clapped and danced a step that was amazing, without any practice. I think it was at that moment, right there under the tree, that we felt liberated from a consciousness that kept following us. The fact that we both were walking into an unknown territory was lingering in our minds but after conquering a small goal, it felt like home already.

There was shade, and there was light.

Of everything, there appeared this golden light that dissipated through the clouds. As we kept walking, it was kissing us in the intervals. The most transforming moments in life don't come with a loud bang, but as silent music that will transcend your senses and question the tense. One such moment was that particular streak of sunlight that held me in its spell. It was inviting as I walked straight up to it.

The leaves were rustling, but this ray was steadying, unperturbed. It gazed back at me equally. You were walking in front. With no one else watching, I bent down, closed my eyes, smelled the warmth of the shine falling on my face, and kissed the ray of light falling on the earth. For a quick second, I opened my eyes and looked upon the falling light to touch my face wholly. I kept my eyes open in the blur of the sun's mirage.

I bent down again, with closed eyes that felt darker inside (the aftermath of looking into the sun). It was just myself and the warm sunlight then, everything else faded. Just the sheer brilliance of the streak of warmth that had travelled from millions of miles away to come all the way and fall on this space and my face. The warm breath of its body, and the sharp sense embraced me, I couldn't help but be consumed wholly in the act of bowing down to its mighty beauty, again, that I could feel with closed eyes.

That was divinity. Destiny.

I smiled, breathed the feeling into me deeply, and from all the life and love inside... I kissed it. It stirred deep as ocean and soft as a leaf. Nothing is stronger than fragility. Nothing is more intense than a kiss. God! It felt so real! I stayed there for an eternity as we kept kissing each other, myself and the warm light, in the realm of the universe that thrived.

The things you do when no one else is watching you, are the real you. That was me, in love. For every reason, you flooded into me as a wave of thought and took centre-stage before I could think of anything else. On the floor, one with the earth, I felt like I was hugged by the land. And then, there was your thought, inevitably, and I tried to extend my hands to reach you. I caught hold of a grass cluster by the side that brought me back to the reality.

I stood up in a jiffy, and you turned back only then to see me altering focus. As much as I was into my own universe, you must have been in yours too, for you didn't care to look back until then. Things that a walk into the woods can do to you, are crazy. I signalled you to continue as if nothing had happened, and paced to keep even with you.

The sun was still up and we managed to cross that terrain. What we saw... I find it hard to describe in words.

✱ ✱ ✱

SHE: (The sight of the waterfall inside the forest)

The trees ended, and it was an open meadow that we found ourselves in. I still can't get that wonderful sight out of my thoughts. The memory is moist in my mind like a raindrop that just fell. The leaves of the trees slowly revealed to us this wide-open view of a waterfall that was thriving right in front of us, not too far, and not so close, either.

We are used to the sight of a multi-storeyed apartment or a mega mall or a frequented flyover. But we are not used to the sight of a waterfall in the middle of a forest that was hustling with the songs of the birds and basking in the light of the sun that was about to set.

That evening seemed longer than a summer. It just stood alive for a long time. In the middle of a distance that was reachable yet remote, there stood a flourishing waterfall. The huge hill in front, the water falling from it, the muffled sound of the crash, the rising sprinkles, the poised rocks, the passionate trees, the purple, orange, and yellow flowers, the welcoming fruits, the chillness in the air, the warmth in the sunshine, the spirit of the forest, and the language of the leaves – everything was felt in the edge of our toes that touched the pebbles that extended until where we were standing.

There was sand and water and fire and wind and the sky. I realized there were the five elements of nature, but also much more than what was seen. There was this unified feeling of getting lost into this sight, as both of us stood perplexed by the sheer nature of nature. It is hard to put in words the kind of emotions that ran through our minds then. You were the first to run forward then, and you took the seat on the rock land that had its share of the sand. I was still standing behind, puzzled on how beautiful it felt to be there.

"Thank you so much! This is something else," I said with a smile that exuded light.

"I feel the same way too. Stunned by this amazing sight, and thankful to be here in this space with you. I mean, this waterfall was always here but it needed a spectator to relish how wonderful it is. It took you and me to come all the way over the greens and the trees to be a part of this. This feels like home," you said with a bigger smile in your eyes.

I walked forward and sat by your side. I took this green view into my eyes, and felt close to peace. There was a rainbow forming right then in the rising water and the sunshine that pierced through. Let us not forego the fact that our hands itched to reach out to a mobile phone and capture this. So many images captured, shared, liked, and stored. Honestly, how often we do we go back and look at these images we shot and stored promptly?

Thankfully, at that time, we had nothing but the thin air to separate us from the mesmerizing view in front of us. Hands rested on the cool pebbles and legs stretched till the brimming water that kept touching our toes sending shrill waves of chillness through the spine, it felt blissful.

I am certainly not someone who travels a lot, or explores the little pleasures of life. You had said so much to me, about how travelling lures the soul into a wandering state of mind, yielding nothing but wisdom. I hadn't really bothered, until that moment when we were in front of that gorgeous waterfall. I couldn't believe that I had walked all the way there. I felt discovered.

* * *

HE: (Jumping into a live water stream)

The horizon of the water touching my feet felt native in a strange way. I kept digging my toes in the rippling water that had its twirl. I moved forward, submerging my legs into the water stream. And then, I laid flat on the rock with grainy sand. The blue sky was dripping orange, and the dragonflies were whirring across. I was wondering if it would rain, but was majorly occupied with the sheer sense of freedom that came with the view of the wide-open sky that was bleeding orange.

Views are important. They give perspectives and yield freshness. This was no normal evening. I was there with you, the one soul that mattered a lot to me, and I was enjoying every bit. It is alarming to see how our smartphones and DSLRs have made us prone to viewing life via the viewfinder, rather than with our naked eye. Back then I realized how amazing and important it is to quit taking pictures and start enjoying the moment. I brought both my hands behind to cushion my head, and rested. I felt like a king, and a kid. A kid is the king of humanity. Then, you peeked in and started speaking with the sky in the background.

"You seem to be really enjoying the moment," you said.

"I am totally in love with this view and this mood," I said adjusting my fingers to the left.

"How I wish I can live in a place like this! Only, I don't know what I will do here to make a living."

"I have had this dream about becoming a farmer too. There is a lot more than this. I am not sure if we will be ready for it…"

"I know. I am just sharing the positive vibe in place. I somehow feel like I belong to this place. Or is it the general nature of any human being to feel so from this sight of the nature?"

"I think we worry too much about making a living. How about not making it, but living it, as it is? Once we are in the river of things and submit ourselves, we will eventually find a way to survive, and then thrive. That is how the entire human civilization has always been, hasn't it? We are not just survivors. We are creatures who thrived. And more than that, we are lovers. I believe we can turn anything around."

"Oh, really? So see this stream of water. Do you think you can jump into it and swim across to the waterfall?"

"When I said the river of things, I meant it metaphorically. Anyway, I truly wish I could jump into this stream. But I don't know how to swim. You know that!

"Of course I do, but as you speak about survival instincts, should you not be able to do it?"

"Oh come on, I wouldn't risk my life for a fact that I would like to defend."

"Men are men!" You smiled.

"But I am not all the men. I am your man!"

You didn't reply to that, but smiled widely, and eclipsed the setting sun in front, for the second time in the evening. But this time, you were up close and I could see the geography of your face. The waves of your hair, the space in your forehead, the pond in your eyes, the sliding hill in your nose, the blooming flowers in your lips... your smile overpowered the light from the sun. I was touched.

This time, I didn't wait to be lifted, but stood up in a jiffy and ran towards the flowing stream of water. And I jumped. I remembered only the splash, and the next second I was drowning. The chillness of the water was frightening and took me by surprise. I wasn't ready for that. I wasn't ready for anything. It was just my instincts, and your face lit with the smile, that made me take the leap to cross the stream.

It was a fast running stream and I couldn't get a hold on anything but my survival instincts were acting fast. I knew I had to live, and cross the stream just for the love of seeing your face in a relieved state. I knew you would be worried, and in the splash of a second, was checking my pocket to see if the car key was with me or you, just in case. The panic moments always usher up the adrenaline in the brain, and the effect is pretty drastic that the body gets equipped magically to combat the situation in dope speed, organically.

The few basic lessons of swimming that I had learnt from my friends and from you came to the rescue from the farthest corner of my memory as I tried swapping my hands and legs to stay above the water that kept taking me forward in its speed. Quickly came the moment where I surrendered and was no longer fearsome. I started understanding the flow of the water and its force. My body automatically adjusted to the critical conditions, and I was gaining control despite the struggle to keep my face above the water.

I was struggling hard so I could keep breathing. Then I figured out that it was not the need to breathe that mattered then but the need to submit and submerge. With a deep breath, I plunged in and used, not my mind but my body to lead me through. I kept my eyes open. That was scary, for all the water hitting my eyes felt surreal. The fins of the fast moving fishes hit my cheeks and as if I got a super power, I let go the fear of the blur and opened my eyes full to see the life underwater.

In the muffled voice of life underwater, I could see the salty images of the water and the corals, and the racing fishes that were more scared to see a stranger in their universe. I truly was wondering what the fishes would be thinking right then, and in the proximity I saw a mass of land sliding up to the surface. I took a swift stroke and let my legs guide me towards it.

Yes, I reached the turf and hit land with a bursting gasp that I didn't know I was missing till then. I grabbed onto the mass of the grass patch that welcomed me to reality. I held it hard, despite its slippery nature, and managed to get my weight over the water. There, I slid on to the patch of land that seemed to save my breath for that minute. I rolled over and laid down facing the sky, gasping for breath.

I could hear your muffled voice through all this, and it felt far yet close. This contradictory feeling of distance always existed between us. The next thing I know, you were there over my face, almost exactly the same way before I took the plunge. Just that, this time you were not smiling, but I could feel the memory of the last smile on your face. I blacked out.

✳ ✳ ✳

SHE: (Blacking out)

The moments when we black out are precious. I mean, how often do we black out? They are the moments when the body takes over the mind, and there is little that you can do about it. It was one of those rare moments when you blacked out. I knew you used to black out when seeing the red of the blood. But to faint to the blues was something that you didn't intend to. I was panicky from the very moment you dived in, and of course, I dived in right after you.

That one-second seemed so long, as it had carried you very far already. I kept my head above and watched you frantically carried away by the flow. I did my best to swim close to you, but you were gone all of a sudden underwater. Imagine the breaths I lost at that moment, and the next moment I was there on the shore, pressing your chest to get you catch your breath.

Everything happened in a whirl. Before I could remember my first aid training to resuscitate an unconscious person, you coughed your lungs out. You were alive. I kept my hands on my face and cried desperately, the panic giving way to a terror that had settled in completely only at that point. I cried aloud. You get to know what someone means to you only in their absence, and this void was fatal, and certainly not what I ever imagined for us.

I wanted to live long together. And I was wondering if I was responsible for you jumping into the water for this antic. You woke up gasping, and kept coughing frantically. For the first time, I felt how important life is.

"Don't worry. I did this on my own" you choked out in between coughs and regaining your conscience.

"But I am worried," I said, my restless eyes looking all over your face.

"I am sorry."

I slapped you hard and shouted out loud, "Do you think this is funny? Did I ask for this? What did you have to prove? What sense does it make to justify something at the cost of your life?"

You replied in an even tone, "I didn't do this to prove anything. I have no need to impress you, for we are far beyond that state of mind where we appreciate surprises more than consent."

"Do you have any idea how I felt when you jumped into the water?"

"Do you have any idea how I felt inside? Let us get the fact out loud that I did this act of stupidity for the way I always love to be an idiot…"

"What if you had drowned? I can't live with that, or after that. Don't you get that part?"

"Come on. Don't forget that my desire to live with you triumphed over the desire to die for you, and here I am, talking to you between broken breaths. This is special. You are special. We are. Let us not dismiss the magic of a new life experience. I just had a new life experience!"

You had a way of putting this forward, and this was certainly too much for me to comprehend. I was finding it hard to accept, and the fact that all of these happened in a matter of seconds made me wonder how slow and fast time can be felt when tested to its limits. Hail Einstein and his theory of relativity. It took a couple of minutes for us to understand that we both were ashore on a small patch of land that was surrounded by water.

It was like an island in the middle of the forest, and the flow of the stream was more than the strength of the survival instincts. There was a tree that stood as our company, within reach. It bore fruits that looked like apples, but then, I don't know. We called it an apple tree anyway. An apple tree in the middle of a solitary patch of land is peculiar. How magical is that? I went forward and plucked a couple of those fruits for you. I sat by your side and gave you an 'apple'.

"This certainly looks like the forbidden fruit, and I don't want to fall from this paradise, ever. Even if there is a fall, let's fall together. Let us take a bite together, shall we?" you asked, with a smile that was so much you.

We bit the apple at the same time, each to their rightful share of the apple. It tasted precious. In the shimmering light, we leaned forward to drink the water from the running stream until we quenched our thirst. We didn't realise that we were thirsty or hungry, until we had that bite of an apple and a sip of the water.

You were still in the water, playing games with it. I came out and was having fun witnessing you do strange things childishly, like the way you held your breath and kept submerged for some time, the way you kept kissing the surface of the water and the way you were staring at your reflection. I didn't want to disturb you. You just came close to being drowned in a free flowing stream.

What can I say? I crawled a step backwards and got a view of our surroundings. We had enough apples and ample water to feed on. A sense of certainty was also crawling along with me. I felt happy to be alive, with you.

* * *

HE: (One of the transforming moments of life)

It was definitely one of the most transforming moments in my life, to have jumped into a live stream of water without knowing how to swim. It was foolish, but most importantly, it was very brave to have taken the risk of trusting the spirit of the human mind. It is all there in the mind, to be able to do or not to anything. I had no point to prove, and no audience to cheer except you who would have been awfully perplexed.

My sole intention was to believe in the moment, which had been magical so far. And it definitely couldn't falter me anymore. Going with the flow, and being with the flow are two different things. Being the flow is altogether a different thing. I intended to be that. I don't know from where I got that super flow of instincts that masked my rational thinking and made me believe in the super power I had.

I have always believed that we all are super powerful; just that it takes a desperate moment to realize that. When I say 'super power' it is not about flying in the sky or travelling at the speed of light, but essential things like the ability to understand failures, the pleasure in letting go, the passion and courage to do what we love, the pursuit to discover the purpose, the sacrifices made for the betterment of self and others, and of course, the grit to jump into a stream without knowing swimming, and more that becomes the sandwich between logic and madness.

There is always a sweet spot, isn't there? And that's the tough spot too. One thing kept startling me. How was I able to see things so clearly and slowly in the twizzle of seconds that slipped through my body creeks? Time slowed down like people said it would when you are high on drugs. I then remembered something I had read in an article long ago regarding the 'fight or flight' moments.

The fight-or-flight response, also called as the acute stress response, is a physiological reaction that occurs in the presence of something that is terrifying, either mentally or physically. Your body triggers a release of hormones to prepare yourself for the combat. Rooting from the choices that our ancient ancestors faced when they encountered a danger in their environment - they could either fight or flee.

The physiological and psychological response to stress in both the cases prepares the body to respond to the danger. I decided to fight. Victory, at times, is not about defeating but about standing the test of time. Endurance was the key. Oh my god, what an experience it was, to look back. It usually takes 20-60 minutes for the mind and body to return to the normal state after such a drastic experience. I was still sinking in the sub-conscious shock.

"How are you so relaxed? I am happy that you are. But this is not the normal you," I said, rubbing both my hands.

"I don't know. I am not usually like this, but I guess I am getting the bigger picture," you said in a confident tone.

"Tone is everything, especially when you don't fake it..."

"Of course, I guess it reflects your intentions and also your confidence. Right now, I am high on confidence. Shoot me a question, I shall answer it sharply."

"What is so special about this evening?"

"Everything, I would say. This very fact that I feel so relaxed is so special.

The more relaxed we are with our self, the more relaxed we are with this entire world. I guess that equates it all."

"Of course. Our state of mind is everything."

"Yours is fast and furious."

"'Yours is slow and steady."

"Absolutely…"

"Certainly!"

"Don't they both mean the same thing – absolutely and certainly?"

"I don't know. 'Absolutely' sounds whole, and 'certainly' sounds partial"

"Whole is made of parts,"

"Like you are made of me,"

"So I am the whole?"

"Maybe."

"Maybe not!"

"Why not?"

"Because we don't know, yet."

"When do we get to know?"

You didn't answer, but reached out, and were holding my hands by then. You came closer to my ground, close to the water. We felt each other intact, but weren't looking at each other. My hold on your hands got firmer to assure ease. It felt different, the decisiveness in the fingers then. It was physical as I could feel every move of our little fingers that seemed altruistic. I had held hands with you and walked so many miles by then, but never had it felt that intense.

Like I said, it was a different mountain of water that kept climbing over my altar of thoughts. Like a sudden change of climate, we were there in the rain of feelings, getting wet with time. It felt really good. The texture of your soft hands, I could feel it all to the detail, and the way we kept rolling our fingers over each other from top to bottom, and changing directions to the left and right too. We kept feeling each other in the setting darkness, and came close to holding each other's fingers in the gaps, and clasping them close but kept missing it voluntarily for the blood to rise and flow to the area of conflict.

We had the entire body at our disposal, but our fingers did not cross the perimeter of the hands. It was so intense that I find it hard to describe now, or to forget, ever.

* * *

SHE: (Eye to eye)

I will never forget the way you held my hands on that shore. It wasn't merely an act but an art where our bodies became totally focused in the kingdom of our hands. It was like our entire senses and sensations were confined to the zone of our hands sliding over each other. It wasn't a firm hold. It was something more than a hold. It was the desire to hold that mattered. Any second we could have held our hands firm and pulled each other close, but the heartbeat of a dream that was not yet realized startled us.

Every time your fingers crossed the life lines on my palms, it sent shock waves inside that dipped my vision into darkness. In a while, I was in a trance, where my eyes weren't really watching what was on the outside but on the inside, picturing the feeling that kept giving birth to a new me. There were a lot of extraordinary moments, the best being those instances when our fingers accidentally and incidentally slipped into the gaps and felt the tightness of the hold that was close by yet far off.

In that proximity, we felt an immeasurable distance that burned so fast that it kept dwindling in the minds. We did give life to that desire, as we let our hands hold tight, with the fingers eclipsing each other's periodically, like once in every ten seconds. It felt whole, when we clinched onto each other in the smallest yet biggest way.

In the order of priority, it is always the legs, hands, and then the face that I give importance to. Hands and legs are selfless. They don't describe any expectations or expect any attention. They keep doing their duty sincerely. I don't remember what our legs were doing. I was numb for many minutes, and wasn't hearing or seeing anything at all until that sound of a flying bird whisking its feathers so close that it shed one on its way.

The lone feather fell down just between us, to touch our fingers that felt like a third person for the first time then. It felt exciting, like an affair that was meant to be. I guess it would have been for an hour or more that we had been hooked by our hands, and this feather in place challenged the commitment. The fact is, the feather was given the due attention, by both of us. I took it off and kept it by the side to make space for us to continue our relationship.

For the first time in many minutes, you looked into my eyes. I wasn't looking at you, but I did feel your sight on my lids. In the fraction of a second I looked at you and felt the sharpness in your eyes piercing right into mine. I have a problem with that, in looking into your eyes when you reflect how much I mean to you in that live black and white film-strip that wasn't rolling, but remained fanatically fixated.

This time I made up mind to give it a fight and kept looking right back into your eyes. Our hands stopped their play, and rested in the green lawn as our eyes did the talking. It is easy to see eye to eye, but to speak eye to eye is extremely difficult, but euphoric. The difficulty only makes the journey longer, and hence sweeter.

In the rumbling sound of the water flowing through the hard rocks, we felt soft in the distance that had an imaginary cotton candy served to each of us. We didn't see it though, for we were engrossed with the moving eyes of each other. I kept moving to the left and right of your vision and kept looking at each of your eye independently, and occasionally together. But you seemed more focused on one single spot of my vision that felt one for both the eyes.

It was like a game of eyes where the hearts were at stake. It felt like the most intense conversation we ever had, as we hit a point where we had our eyes glued, and it was a bridge of love that kept building itself between us. Our bodies didn't move, it felt so moving. I melted like cotton candy taking a dip in the flowing water.

The light was disappearing marvellously. The light lit the earth for one last time that day. The ball of life was falling right into the waterfall that was brimming with love, splashing water that kept touching our feet forts on the moist soil. The trees around were being embraced by the golden light, and were in total submission. You could say it in their movement that they considered this moment special. The golden rays then poured themselves into the flowing river, and were dispersed as the yellow mercury that fell apart. The light of the darkness slowly started setting in.

✳ ✳ ✳

HE: (Kissing your forefinger)

The evening was getting darker, and the night was yielding a wisdom, pure and passionate. The sound of the waterfall, the flowing river, and the dancing trees became a norm and we were no longer intimidated by the stunt of a new place. We felt like we belonged. In the middle of all these thoughts engulfing us, I raised (y)our hands until your face and broke the chain of communication we had. It was getting too intense, and also too close to a collapse of the emotions. I didn't want either of us to lose or win for that matter. I loved the conflict of eyes till then, and the adrenaline rushed to the hands as we were connected again.

I came closer, and as I moved forward, my toes touched the chill stream beneath. The rising water reached out to me, and I was pleasantly surprised to feel its chillness. I retreated my legs and focused on catching the same nerve of surprise in your territory as I moved an inch closer with resistance. We were close enough to cut all the wires of consciousness, but far enough that we still waited for it to happen.

I placed my face on yours with our noses touching each other, and we tried to look into each other's eyes. It was dark and too hazy in that closeness to get a clear picture, but who cares? Blur is beautiful. And rare. With a deep breath, I took myself in and let myself out. Your breath touched my lips. And it wasn't by chance, was it? Nothing really happens by chance. It was meant to happen and it happened.

Like the mind stretching after reading a book, my senses were elastic after feeling your breath. I sunk my forehead deeper onto yours, and rested my breath on yours. I didn't move a bit after that. The warmth of the breath took over us. And I wasn't able to move my thoughts beyond its spell. It is a different kind of feeling to breathe your loved one's breath.

Those are the moments when you are completely detached from everything else. But the moment called now… It thrives. Right then, in the middle of an unknown forest that teemed in its glory, there we were, in front of a waterfall and exchanging breaths. Life is beautiful, isn't it?

I moved back and watched your face glisten in the moonlight. I could see the reflection of running water on your face that remained flawless like the moon above. There were two full moons, in front of me and up above too. You smiled at me in a way that only I could understand. We locked eyes and stayed in the trance of our vision. It was one, our vision, and it saw nothing but the vulnerable us melting in each other's heat, and dying to stay together as long as we could, even if it meant that little bridge of life between our eyes.

We have always longed to be together, this way, with just nature around us. For a moment, we started hearing all the sounds from around us – the rustling of the leaves, the gushing of the water, the chirping of the insects, the rousing of the hills, the calm of the moon, and finally, the music of our breath overpowering everything else. I held your hand, took it closer to my lips, but leaped onto kiss your forefinger with a certainty stronger than any I had ever felt.

✳ ✳ ✳

SHE: (The print of a kiss on the paper of consent)

The print of your kiss landed deep into me, and I felt like a driftwood floating on your waters, waiting to be made into papers. The weight of a wet paper took a temporary abode in my mind. 'Take me with you', I whispered inside.

"Are you feeling cold?" You asked in a concerned tone. I know you cared for me, always.

"It is only you that I can feel now. I know my teeth are chattering. But I guess it shows how nervous I am," I said in a lost yet true tone. I wasn't dramatic or romantic, but just me being honest.

"Can we cross this little stream of water and go a little closer to the waterfall?" You asked abruptly.

That was the last mile. I couldn't see a thing but didn't care to, either. I had no idea about how far we were set to go, or how deep the water was. Leaving back all the precious memories we held there was the most dreadful part, as we slid into the stone cold water and gathered each other in our hands to walk swift and straight towards our goal. We didn't speak for a few seconds as our teeth wrote their own scripts out of the chillness in the water.

"This is cold. Like the indifference of the geography teacher whom I hated in school," you said, and kept moving faster than me.

"I am doing this for you," I said with a typewriting pause between every word through the teeth.

Words had no purpose as we combated the cold of the water. Somehow we kept feeling the depth of the water every now and then. It was not years, or months, or weeks, or even days... It was the very next second that accounted to our definition of the future.

The water level had reached our hips. You let go of my hand for a brief second and kept walking. Once again, before I could ask you about it, you came up with this inspiring question, "Can we have a race now?"

How absurd is that in the middle of a slow flowing river in a lonely forest when the only choice is to keep the head above water?

"Over there, see, that green patch of land in between, is what I am talking about," you continued, with a committed body language that was visible even in the darkness. I did not ask a thing, but extended my hands onto yours. You smiled for my consent, and after my consent too.

✳ ✳ ✳

HE: (Sleeping with you)

Why would anyone offer his or her hand after accepting to race? But we did, holding hands and racing together. It was very hard to run through that cold and heavy stream of slow water. Also, it was a very different kind of race where victory was guaranteed to both the competitors. In fact, there was no competition but the act of co-existence, just like how nature and wildlife co-exist, it was just you and I running with struggling breaths and firmly held hands.

The water level was kissing our chest by then, and our eyes were taking in the splatter of our rush as we closed eyes occasionally but didn't lose the balance. All the matters of perseverance and trust pay. Ours did too, then, as we started feeling a descent in the water level all of a sudden. It went down slowly and crawled almost until the knees. It gave us confidence. We were able to move faster. Our legs were our eyes then, as we kept searching for the shore to seek us.

We then hit the sand bed ascending up. There we bumped together with a free fall onto the ground that awaited us. The shore awaited us, and we were breathing, vehemently filling the void that we had in the uncertain act of crossing a cold river at that point of time. Our hearts were pounding faster, and we were crawling our fingers into the sand to feel the soft grains that held us home, then. Home is where you feel belonged and alive. Right then, under the shade of the skies and the light of the moon, we felt home in the forest of ourselves. I dragged you closer, to imprison you with the freedom in my warmth.

"That does feel warm, thank you," you said with a smile that I felt was warmer than our cuddles.

"I accept your thanks. I am not going to dismiss it as formality," you said with an even bigger smile that felt even warmer.

"It is nice when you actually accept a note of thanks that is meant sincerely. I guess it is perfectly fine to express and accept gratitude. It just is as simple as that."

"There are no formalities, at least between you and me. In fact, there is no normalcy either. As in, how often do two souls decide to walk into a random forest for the fun of it, cross treacherous terrain, find a waterfall, want to get closer, and end up crossing a cold river that took their breath away at various instances?"

"Maybe there are. Like you and me, there could be many more souls doing crazier things."

"And more insane…"

"And the impossible…"

"Nothing is impossible!"

"Everything that is real now was once only dreamt about."

"Dreams do come true."

"I am feeling all the more new."

"I am feeling you!"

"I don't know what to say…"

"There is nothing to say. Everything is understood…"

"You are my soul companion,"

"You are my sole companion!"

"Just close your eyes, and hear my heart reaching out to you."

I tugged you closer, and kept your face on my chest that had the beat of the heart, and the warmth of the earth. Your face was buried in my chest, and you adjusted your ears closer to my chest. We didn't speak a thing but kept reading the sentences of the warmth our bodies were writing into us. I kept caressing your wet hair and you kept stroking my ears. There was no hurry. No fear. And no concept of time. There was only the space that held us in its ground. Like the melting note of a violin sinking us in its depth, we slipped into a state of sleep, even before our eyes were fully closed.

Chapter 9.5

When Souls Make Love

"All the exhaustion of the evening came to the ground as those two souls paused in peace in a tempestuous calming night," said the blue star.

"It feels musical, to see them sleep like this. I mean, look at them! She is resting on him, and he is resting on her. The intimacy of genuine companionship is far more sensational than the surge of lust, isn't it? I am losing track of the tense. It feels like the present, still" said the pink star with a wink.

"It was really overwhelming to see how the entire forest was looking at them then. The environment paid attention to these two souls who were totally naked to anything around, and were experiencing a trip that mattered."

"I love the way they slept instantly, feeling content without really having to prove anything at all to each other!"

"I guess they proved a lot already."

"Yes, I agree."

"It definitely didn't look easy is what I feel."

"What's the fun in feeling easy?"

"Or playing easy?"

"Play is the highest form of research, said Einstein!"

"Are you kidding?"

"I am just playing!"

"I meant that, too. I just enjoy pulling the words out of your twinkle! Ha!"

"What happens now?"

"You know it…"

"But I am not going to say it!"

"Yes, for it has to be felt."

"How beautiful can a night get?"

"More beautiful! The night always gets better."

✳ ✳ ✳

They were sleeping. There was no time in place, so we can't really tell how short or long it was. They just slept. Imagine a life like that, where you are not bound by time but only the needs in your space. The need to rest, the need to work, the need to eat, and the need to do everything else… It's like you will eat only when you are hungry, and sleep only when you are tired. It solves a lot of our problems, doesn't it?

But actually it is set to create more problems. I mean, what will happen to the appointments scheduled, the restaurant's timings, the alarm's purpose, and everything that is a part of the plan? We are all in a plan revolving around time and we can't help checking the time. Individually the magical act of forgetting time and living a need-based life is rebellious, and most importantly, possible. But as a community, it is hard to accomplish. As a company of two, it may be achievable.

A lot like how these two souls were able to achieve. He and she, we all know where they started their fight. And look where they are now, resting in the memory of each other's shoulders, and their far away stars are sparkling at them with more shine than the moon up close. The universe kept supporting as these two souls forgot everything in the trance of sleep, and drifting as a sight that the trees around relished.

To see two souls submitted to earth was an absorbing sight for them. The sum of their silence added to become a lump of thoughts in his throat that gave him a cough, which woke her up. She slowly opened her eyes, but couldn't immediately relate to where she was. It took a few seconds for her to cut through the darkness and see where she really was. The grip of his hands was still there, and she didn't escape that but created a small distance so she could see him in that gleaming moonlight.

It is beautiful to watch people sleeping, for that is when you get to see their real self, devoid of anything at all. They are alive and also dead at the same time, for they don't control their thoughts, but their thoughts control them. She kept watching his eyes that were rolling beneath the closed lids. She thought he must be having a dream, and didn't want to disturb him.

Taking a very calculated step, freeing herself from his clutches, she went a little further away, still in the warmth of his self, and kept looking at him like she always did. She leaned forward slightly, and placed her fingers on his face. She started to disturb the hair on his forehead. He never liked anybody messing with his hair, including her. Because it is forbidden, it felt all the more pleasing to her as she kept fiddling with his hair and smiled out of her sleepy eyes.

She was all-awake, and was hearing the rush of the water in the rinse of the skies being reflected. She sincerely kept stroking his hair, partly because she had the liberty to, and also because she believed that it would wake him up. She needed him. She wanted him. Both were the same to her, the need and the want. Being a man of words, he always expressed more and won her over intensely, but what's more powerful then, is her silence that won over the words and the poems and all the prose he had ever written. Her words were not written but felt. Her weaknesses are her strengths. Her vulnerability was so real that it imparted an intense vibe that traversed through his skin.

It was a colossal moment as he opened his eyes slowly, responding to the weight of her forefinger. He lost sleep and found her in his sight. She was looking at him. It didn't take long as he locked eyes with her instantly, cupped her face and kept looking into her eyes. There was not even an interval of seconds, but his subconscious took control over him. The wetness had gone, but the chillness prevailed, and he tugged her closer and saw a blur. How lovely is this blur? He didn't intend to be distracted by the blur but instead felt its bliss intentionally. She was then resting on the same shoulder, but in a different way, where she wasn't hearing his heartbeat, but was feeling the same. Neither of them was sleeping, but they were in a state of trance between dream and reality. More like the hour just before the night ends and the morning begins, lively yet dormant, it was that magical bridge between the conscious and the subconscious that was hit by the waves of each other's self.

The trance kept building up to the moment where they were prepared to lose their individual identities. With a sigh that settled all the questions, he cupped her face, again, but this time to come closer to her breaths that he loved the most. The breath is the bridge between the inside and the outside. Nose on nose, with just the space to let them contemplate the warmth, he rested his breath on hers, again. She rested hers on his.

They were in an agreement inked with serendipity.

In a while, they adjusted their faces so that they were breathing in each other's breaths completely. Like a spell hard to break, they kept inhaling each other into their selves, and the heat burnt the distance with every sigh. They could have kissed, yet they kept yearning. He consciously took a minute to hold the back of her head calmly, and felt the texture of her hair. There were sand grains sprinkled all over her hair and body, naturally after sleeping on the sand for so long that neither of them knew.

An important moment in their life was being authored. It was not the creator who was in control, but the creation that took control. The creators were led by the creation as they started rising to each other in a trance that was hard to explain. He kept holding a different part of her every time she slid her hair through his fingers. He rolled over to sit up straight, resting on the lonely tree that was close to his back. She sailed along with him past the earth, and reached out to him.

She was sitting in front of him as he held her hands, smelled her nails, and kissed her fingers. He wasn't sure if it was the forefinger or the middle finger or all of them, but he was sure he was kissing her hands like he'd kiss her face. He saw her everywhere. She was submitting herself charmingly to the act of love, and was feeling high in herself.

A man can never understand how it feels for a woman to be high. It is like trying to translate the language of the river. Women are perennial souls.

Only women and the soil are capable of giving birth to another life on this earth. His lips kept writing a story of love in the path that ascended from the fingers. Every single inch seemed like a separate universe that he wanted to come back later to explore.

When he kissed her wrist, she dwindled like a clock's second-hand ticking. When he kissed her elbow, she raised her head and rested it back where it was. When he kissed her biceps, she breathed out a different sigh than the earlier one that seemed in control. When he kissed her shoulder, she almost broke a bone inside as she swiftly retreated to let loose the mass of senses that seemed too heavy to be held in one single place.

The scattered senses travelled all over her body, and were between places that were hard to locate. The movement of their bodies was limited and special, as they made changes in the latitude and longitude to come closer to each other. They were so close already, yet had a lot of distance in between to travel, especially when lips were the ones doing the trip. He kept kissing her shoulder like scissors biting paper – not so fast, yet so sharp – precisely scissoring to the silver lining of her neck.

The neck, oh god, the neck. What is it about the neck that dances so much when kissed? Never had she been as nervous as she was when he climbed over to her neck, holding her spine in one hand and the back of her head in another and kissed her neck. An ocean of sensations engulfed her, letting her drown in the doped ride as she attempted hopelessly to gain some hold. It felt like a slippery slide downhill for her, to hold on to anything on the way down as every bit of her crumbled when he planted the foundation of his kisses strong in her neck.

In the smiling curve of her neck, he continued to explore the infinite possibilities of love that were becoming tangible. He went over to hold her ears in the cusp of his lips, and uttered a musical chord of breath that didn't read a meaning, but meant everything that needs to be said. He took a deep breath and exhaled into her ears that kept crying susceptibility across the endless borders.

There were no borders, yet powerful invisible lines that came as a surprise every time they were crossed. They tripped over it for the love of falling. And when they fell, they rose. They fell and rose, in love. He lowered his shoulder to make some space for her to come closer, as he tugged her up unto him, this time heart to heart, shoulder to shoulder, and hugging her safe into his self.

She felt safe, and endangered at the same time. To feel his heart's beat this close was not something she could take in easily. It was different. He breathed heavily and she did too, relatively more. Slowly and steadily he hugged her again, but with a different stab on the back that left a scar in her soul for the first time in the night. She crawled past the sand that her feet struggled to come through.

They were available. The act of being available is an art. Submission is supremacy, and not easily attainable. There was submission and surrender, unanimously. It was not about who was more powerful, but who was more vulnerable. The success lied in defeat.

How enticing is it to lose? In love, it is.

In the music of Beethoven's moonlight sonata, like a leaf that fell from its branch to the earth, his kiss made its way over her face. It touched her soft eyes that closed like a curtain drawing, her nose that came forward with a slow and long breath that carried her confidence, her cheeks that turned softer, her ears that heard the whispers of the leaves nearby that were watching them in love, her chin that held the rhythm of resistance in place.

A sudden breeze tossed her hair and washed her face with chillness, but the warmth of his breath stood alone, felt profoundly. Everything that there was led to the lips that waited the most dramatic collapse of senses. The wait was savoured, as he felt the softness of her cheeks by hand, and they kissed. The tender feeling when you lay on a bed was there as he slowly, steadily, rested his lips on hers.

As a flower that inhaled its holder, she went onto kiss his lips in a way that defied his belief in everything else. His feet felt light as he struggled in vain to handle her reaction, and reply. High on love, they were in rippled waters then as they moved on kissing each other equally, taking turns.

They were swapping kisses, up and down, and feeling each other in a different way with every kiss. He was feeling her shoulder, and she was feeling the back of his head. He was feeling her neck, and she was feeling his hips. Their hands were undertaking a journey by themselves. And the legs, they kept pushing the ground to get closer to each other. There was no direction to go but into each other, as they kept kissing crazily.

What started gentle turned passionate, and close to madness as they lost sight and saw only the music that the lips spilled past their breaths. She bit his lips. With sharp pain, he retreated, only to fall upon her shoulder and rise with a breath to her neck and bite her passionately. They were printing love tattoos on each other. The second skin was no longer needed. And as he tried to unveil her blue top, she was raising her hands already, in the hissing of the hills in front.

And then, she vehemently pulled over his pink t-shirt, and threw it by the side of the bed that was burning in their lust. The thrown clothes had their destiny as they found their places where they were meant to be. Untying everything else they wore, they were naked in front of the dreamy waterfall. He sat up straight, and hugged her wholly. They were tied in their arms, reaching out to each other's back in the hug as their legs kept calling each other closer in their clasp.

He kissed intensely, and she kissed immensely. The blanket of the skies slowly dissolved as the first light entered the foliage and touched their senses. The birds had started their dawn's chorus, and here, on Earth, are these two souls making love to each other. He kissed her chest and she kissed his ears. He kept kissing her intensely, and she raised her head to the sky's ceiling in a reverie letting go of his hair strands that slipped like water seeping through the rocks.

Rolling over the sand of dreams, and the bed of memories, they were frolicking as one in the middle of a teeming forest and a steamy bedroom. They were alive and awake in both the worlds. The past and the present were one. They were one. The leaves were rustling, and the curtains were crumbling. Encompassed by the door of the terrain, and the window of water, there they were sandwiched in a latitude that forgot its longitude.

Just when they lost their directions, he took her by storm and lifted her in his hug as she held onto him tightly, with her legs crossed around his back. He kept kissing her, and the room had enough space for a forest to come alive between them. The worlds were merging, the souls were merging, and so were their bodies. He walked along, holding her tight, lifting her weight, yet feeling so light in the demesne of the kiss that carried them both through.

He took a round to hit the wood of the lonely tree to rest his back on the wooden bark, and she held the handle of the cupboard to get a hold of the moment she was falling in love with him. The sum total of their weight at that moment was less than that of the individuals' added together. A large portion of their weight was shared with the air, where love took residence.

Gravity failed. Logic failed. God damn what is this love anyway that is driving the souls and the bodies crazy? What is love, after all?

Definitions kept appearing in the way they looked into each other's eyes at regular intervals, only to kiss each other passionately. She seemed to have most of the control then, as she was resting on him. It was an amazing moment to live through. Touch wood, they did, literally. And with a swing, she pulled back to bring him closer to the bed of sand as he held her falling self to land safe in the quilt of time. They took their time to breathe easy, and took the space to feel closer.

In the structure of the sand, and the softness of the quilt, they kept moving with the slightest effort as a cloud would move past its present place. They had been in the blanket of darkness so far, but the clouds were breaking free to shower the first signs of light. They sat up again, face to face, looking at each other as the shades of light playing with layers of colours kept kissing their faces. It was different. It felt new. Everything felt new.

He looked at her as if it was the first time, and she nodded, acknowledging how beautiful the first time always is. He smiled, she cried. In his smile trickled a tear, and amidst her tears tripped out a smile. As the sky was painted close to orange, light was livening up their little cottage. Dispersed sand, wrinkled bed sheets, singing birds, whirling fan, the whimsical waterfall, the standing water bottle, the tall trees, the teak bed... everything was in sync and the parallel worlds were one. They were one.

She parted her the hair on her forehead so she could feel the light of the skies and the warmth of his eyes vividly. He helped her set aside the hair flirting with her forehead. Their bodies shone in the first light of the morning, and the sun was about to break through, given the orange glitter it sprinkled all over. They placed their hands on each other's chest and felt the heart beating to the magic that was happening. There is no landscape as beautiful as the human body, and the light travelled through every curve of them.

It was pure, and placid, as he leaned forward to kiss her on her forehead. She closed her eyes and so did he. Their eyes were wide open in all the darkness they had embraced till then, but the moment the light came in, they closed their eyes and entered a different kind of vision. They saw each other in the way it felt inside. The lips kept kissing, the rasping fingers ran restlessly all over the body, cutting loose yet catching a grip. The dying breath lived to die again, the rubbing shoulders oozed music in vain, the subtle skin got subtler, the breaking bones got more brittle, the salty sweat reflected the morning skies, and the exuding heat melted the morning ice...

The universe was watching them as they reached down to earth and felt a rebirth. Love is Mother. Love is Earth. No wonder why it felt so natural to fall back on the earth with their skin sinking into the sand as they rolled over. In the inch of his reach, he tripped down the water bottle that leaked, and she felt the splash of the lively stream in reach as the water dappled her face.

The body is the most magical thing that there is. Made up of trillions of cells, atoms, and molecules... and of stories, dreams, and memories, it is all we got. Life resides in the bodies. Souls co-exist with the bodies. Our bodies are our homes. It was homecoming then, as they opened their bodies to each other. In the subtle curves of her body, and the strong lines of his, there happened a coincidence that was meant to be. Locked in love, that first wave of trance that swept them through their bodies was unexplainable.

They struggled to breathe but managed to, eventually. Up and down, to and fro, naked in the sun's beam past the clustered clouds and the covered blankets, they kept feeling each other as deep as they could.

There were no limits. There was no agenda. Just the precipitous feeling of love that kept building inside and outside that equally mattered. For many minutes that didn't warrant an explanation, they were lying in this forest room and making love like the leaves and the breeze would.

Changing positions, they continued to make every second count. Before a minute was over, they had lived an hour already. Before an hour was over, they had missed the minute already. A lot of what happens when souls make love is unexplainable.

The sensation was spread, and was due as per its destiny. The clouds broke free, as the souls moved in a way that complemented their bodies. Neither of them wanted to stay in control then. They surrendered to the magic of the unknown. He was almost on the verge of falling but held on to her rising fall in progress. He was the tree, and she was the waterfall. It felt like many years that they had spent together in the minute moments of pleasure in progress.

In the loudest of her senses, she exploded like a river breaking its course. He burst into her spontaneously like a boundless river finding its force. They hit the moon together as they trembled in pleasure lit by the sun's rise to be seen as a silhouette by the stones in front. They didn't give in, but were in the dance of the cosmos for quite some time, after which she fell down on him with one last ocean of breath.

Both of them were breathing heavily. The music of their breaths conquered everything else. Their bodies were inhaling and exhaling in sync. When she exhaled, he inhaled. When he exhaled, she inhaled. Right there, in the bed of the forest, with the first light piercing through the leaves and the window, there they stayed tugged into each other in a way that is far lovelier than what could be imagined. There laid the two souls who were in love with each other, not for any other reason but the sheer cause of existence.

They loved. They breathed. They exist.

Chapter 10

The Beginning

The night that started with them lying on their bed with sands of memories, ended in the same place but in a different position of thought - in the minds and the bodies. She was smiling with eyes closed as he leaned on her neck and rested his breath. And they talked without a resistance.

"It felt like a dream," she said catching the breath she had lost until then.

"And it did come true," he said, closing his eyes, putting his hands around her neck, and smiling in sync with her.

"I don't know where or how it started, it just feels like a faraway dream that came so close. I am still not in terms with the reality of it."

"Exactly, it felt like I was here but also not here. It was like… I was here, but it felt like I was elsewhere too, in a faraway place, if you know what I mean…"

"I totally get it, because I feel the same way too, like a shared dream."

"A shared dream? That's fascinating."

"Is it even possible?"

"I have my questions too, like why we started to fight, and how we ended up here, in each other's arms."

"Come on. You can't say you didn't know why we started the fight. Wasn't it the coffee table that you hated?"

"Or the coffee table you loved? I guess we can put it both ways."

"But it was never about the coffee table, was it? It was about everything else that surrounded it. God! That was a good fight"

"I agree to what you said last night. I feel it is important that we fight often. I am not going to shy away from it anymore. Let me hit the ice off my head. We had made love many times, but this time felt different."

"There is no winner in the game of love, but victory lies in participation. We don't participate anymore, but want to win all the time, don't we?"

He kept holding her hands close to his chest all the time, and kissed her fingers with a soothing weight that she felt on her ears. She held their hands together, and kissed him back in her fingers that met her lips first. It didn't matter, for it felt mutual.

"I don't know exactly how long, but it feels like so long ever since we had an open conversation," she said with an open smile, bringing their hands held together on her chest.

"I guess we have all the time in the world, but we don't have the mind anymore. We don't have the mind to be in this space where we can talk. Of course we talk every day, but not in this zone of conversation where nothing else matters but being listened to."

"Come closer, and rest all your worries on me. I want to bear it all. You are a fever that heals me…"

"Sounds revolutionary. I hear music now, being played with a tribal instrument by Australian aboriginals. And there is a hum of the drums too. Where are we?"

"I believe we are in a forest of thoughts which needs no explanation. The forest needs no explanation. When you are in a forest there are no comparisons or privileges. You simply are close to your roots, and to nature. You are simply yourself."

"I am not drunk, but I feel high, genuinely."

"I am drunk, in the ocean of your thoughts. I am drowning in it, like right now. But there's no struggle to breathe. I'm breathing just fine."

"I can hear you breathe. The sound of it touches me far more than anything else. I can feel my breath too, and it feels magical to pay attention to the breathing. It is something we keep doing all the time, a proof of our life. God, I love the way you breathe."

"I love the way you said it."

"I meant it."

"I know."

"You better do…"

"Of course!"

"What else?"

"I don't know, you tell me."

"What's up?"

"It is the usual question that I get every day from so many people. And it is one of the hardest things in this world… replying to the question 'What's up?'"

"I agree. Agreement is beautiful when meant without a signature, and between hearts and minds."

"Now you tell me, what's up?"

"I guess the ceiling to start with, and there are the skies, and the clouds. And far beyond, there are the stars that will still keep staring at us. Because we don't see them doesn't mean they don't see us. Somehow, I feel they always see us. They are our shadows in the skies!"

He hugged her closer, but still there seemed to be a space that can be reduced. Nothing else was needed. The emptiness is the wholeness. That's where the beauty lies. What makes the pot, a pot? The emptiness! What makes the sentence, a sentence? The space between the words! Take anything in life and it will be the space that brings meaning to it, not the content that is being populated into it, or perceived from it. They understood the importance of it.

They understood the importance of giving the space that is needed to feel strange, and new. They didn't speak it out loud, no. But they felt the essence of it. They felt the essence of space, one that exists out there in the cosmos, and continues to startle. They kept cuddling and caressing each other. Words cannot suffice to express the feeling of being hugged after making love, and staying with the present.

Gifted are the souls that enjoy a cup of conversation after making love.

They were gifted. They kept talking, not just through words but through the hold they had on each other's bodies. Bodies talk, as much as our voice does. Call it lust. What is love without lust, or lust without love?

"I feel belonged with you. It's beyond time and distance. I've always felt belonged when conversing with you. It is a dream come true to be realizing this now. It is like a book coming alive," he said.

"How special is that. Thank you. I feel very proud of you. I will strive to deserve your affection. This is amazing. I want a copy of this book that we have authored now," she said.

"You will always have my love. You already do. You are a perennial river of goodness. I will make you prouder. I don't know why I am saying this, but I feel truly proud in saying this, too. I will make you prouder. I still remember the fragrance of the sea in the poems you had secretly written during the college days. It remains etched in my heart, not just as a memory but also more as a dream. Blessed are souls who yearn!"

"Everything you are saying is so magical to me. As if I am struck by a giant diamond tuning fork that magically resonated with my soul, I feel your vibe. You always have a yearning. And it doesn't warrant an end but only the beginning..."

"Destination is a beginning!"

"You are amazing. You are. We are two less lonely people now."

"Your eyes speak more than you think"

"God, you are a soul that grows younger. You know that, right? Face is the index of the mind they say, looking at your face right now with cupped hands and fixed eyes, all you seem to do is to grow younger. You are a gift. You are a blessing. Quickly touch your cheeks and tell me you feel what I say?"

"I do. This is what I call oddities of fate. How is it that, in this entirely heartless absurd world, there is someone who can sing to my soul?!"

"This wave of feelings... It's magical. And it's real too. How beautiful is that? I can hear you breathe."

"It has been a rough phase yesterday and for a few days. Your words, your love... your energy, your joy, and the way you choose the words to convey it... all of this is rearranging the structure and meaning of my universe right now. I was feeling a little beaten up from not being able to give anymore... I needed to take. And from you, I take this moment!"

"I am so happy for you, and happier still that you are lifting me up right now. Thank you!"

"I feel lifted too. I feel like the way you lift your child, and feel lifted in the process. I don't know how else to explain how close and real I feel right now."

"Hard to explain, but worth the effort too. Whatever hardships you face, always remember this - you are more than that!"

"You are special. You are true. You are an angel. It is fine to flutter a little. You tend to, when flying. That's how you fly. That's how angels fly."

"Thanks! I can fly with broken wings too!"

"You will always fly, for you are not just a bird but a song. A song needs no wings."

"I am reading this again and again in my mind, this page of our conversation, this chapter of our life. Thank you!"

"By far, this is the most powerful conversation we've had, maybe of all I've had of late with anyone else too. It moves, and it just stirs. And I feel belonged. There are people and things that you are comfortable with. And there are souls whom you feel belonged to. I am sure you understand."

"I understand you without an explanation..."

"I feel belonged!"

"I feel love between two strangers. In all the familiarity,"

"I will definitely see you the way I see you now, always. I truly hope so. I have an ocean in my eyes when I say this, which is reflected in the tear that finds its way down. It trickles down and kisses my cheek. My vision is blurred now, but I can see clearly. I see happiness. I see you. I see love. I see goodness! Sigh..."

"I am smiling big with tears trickling down. I truly am smiling my widest, and it shakes me up to be in this state of joy. How can your calm give me this stirring? The joy of being understood..."

Oh,

My!

You!

Who are you?

What are you?

"I feel a high that no drug could ever top. Thank you!"

"What is being told is only the surface, but what's being felt is the untold, and the unknown. You are brimming with it. When you write, I feel like I am being read. I feel like a book in your hands right now."

"I need you"

"I want you"

"I love you"

"I love us"

"I feel I am meeting you for the first time"

"How is this even possible?"

"Everything is possible, between you and me."

Made in the USA
Monee, IL
07 July 2026

56555694R00121